Hood Love & Loyalty

By: B

"Love does not begin and end the way we seem to think it does. Love is a battle, love is a war; love is a growing up."

~~~ James Baldwin

Larissa

The sound of my alarm going off caused me to wake up way too early. I hated mornings. But I hated living in this house more thanks to my racist ass stepdad. The thought of his ass made me want to hurry up and get ready for school, even if it was early as hell. I hoped to only be living here for a few more months. I needed a place to stay until I graduated, and I wasn't gonna let my dislike for his ass mess that up for me. So I would continue to keep my mouth shut and put up with his ass in the meantime.

I always tried to keep my emotions in check anyway so a few more months wouldn't hurt. One of the lessons I learned when I was younger was that if you show a weakness of any kind somebody will use that against you down the road. I guess you could say that trust didn't come easy for me and I was okay with that. You couldn't get hurt if you didn't let anyone in.

I was eighteen years old and a senior in high school. The last seven months had been a rollercoaster for me. Right before my senior year of high school I made the decision to up and move hundreds of miles away from home. I wanted to get away from my father and have a closer relationship with my mother. Of course even family can't always be counted on. When I got here and shit didn't work out the way I hoped, I wasn't surprised. The truth was I was alone in the world and had known it for a long time.

I grew up in Chicago. Not in the hood like most people think of when they find out I'm from there. My

4

father made sure the streets didn't taint me or at least the image he was trying to portray. Which was crazy to me since he came from the same place he tried to keep me away from.

I was what most people considered a "bad bitch". Everyone thought I looked exotic which was the result of being mixed. I didn't put much value on my looks though and being the pretty girl was more of a curse than a blessing.

I was always seen as an outsider and had to learn early on how to defend myself against hating ass bitches. I would usually let that shit roll off my shoulders unless some bitch really tried me. I wasn't like those stuck up females that acted like they were better than everyone just because they were pretty. I never let the way I looked get in the way of how I treated people.

I pushed the covers back and stood up stretching in the process. I went to my dresser and grabbed my clothes for the day. I chose to wear a pink tank top, a pair of ripped skinny jeans, and some Jordan's. I always liked to be comfortable and cute. I wasn't all into name brands, wearing lots of jewelry, or being over the top. I did wear a little makeup but kept it mostly natural.

After a quick shower I dried my hair adding some coconut oil conditioner which left my natural curls defined and soft. Today I put on some foundation and mascara. Then I sprayed my favorite fragrance from bath and body works all over. I looked at my reflection in the mirror and was satisfied with the result. When I finished getting ready it was time for me to head to school.

I pulled out the keys to the old crown Vic I was allowed to drive thanks to my mother's red neck husband. The car even had a Harley Davidson sticker posted on the back windshield. It was a piece of shit but I didn't complain because it got me where I needed to go and I didn't have a job to buy a better one. My focus was getting good grades and graduating so I could go to college next fall and get the hell out of this house ASAP. So for the time being the car would have to do.

I pulled into the school parking lot and found an open spot near the back. As I put my car in park another car pulled in beside me. It was a dark blue Altima with tinted out windows that I had never seen before. I went ahead about my business picking up my purse and books and opened my car door to get out. As soon as I opened my door it was hit by the other car's door being opened at the same time.

This was not how I wanted to start my day off. But I wasn't one to hold onto shit that happened. I didn't really care if there was any damage to the car I was driving anyway. The whole thing was irritating more than anything especially when the boy who did the shit got out. His ass looked down at me still standing there and laughed.

"Damn shorty watch what you're doing next time."

I wasn't feeling his joke especially because it was still too early for that shit. I rolled my eyes and slammed the door shut instead of going back and forth with the nigga. I recognized him from the basketball team but didn't know his name or anything.

I began to walk away so I wouldn't be late for my first class. After a few steps I looked back over my shoulder. Both the driver and the nigga who hit my door were now standing there watching me walk away with their eyes glued to my ass.

"My bad. Have a good day!" I said with a genuine smile on my face.

I know they were wondering what the fuck I was thinking or why I would tell them have a good day after what happened. Especially after I gave that dirty ass look, but I was over the shit already. When I told them to have a nice day I meant it and I planned to do the same no matter how it started out.

I turned back around and tried to slow my pace down to catch my breath. Whoever that man was standing next to the nigga who hit my door, had my head fucked up from the way he was staring at me.

He was like no other man I had ever seen before. I didn't even know who he was but there was just something about him that caught my attention. I wasn't trying to get caught up with any nigga any time soon no matter how fine he was. I would probably never see his ass again though so there was no harm in lusting over him a little bit.

Messiah (Money)

In these streets I'm known as an up and coming boss. My family name holds a lot of power and mothafuckas know not to fuck with me. Ever since my oldest brother got picked up by the feds last fall I've been heavy in the streets trying to find out who the snitch was on his team. I can't stand a disloyal ass nigga. Someone who will smile in your face and turn around and do all that talking to the police just like a bitch. I got no love for police or those who talk to them period.

I was dropping my little brother Maurice off to school and he hit some girl's car door when he was getting out. It didn't seem to do any damage to the car since it was already in bad shape otherwise I would have offered to pay for the shit.

Shorty was bad as fuck too. Her body was out of this world and my dick bricked up instantly. She had long ass legs I could see myself wrapped between.

I don't even know why I was thinking about her ass since this was the first time I had even seen shorty. I definitely wasn't a nigga to wife a bitch, but I would love to see what the pussy was like. I was too young for that relationship shit and plus I had a baby on the way with a crazy ass baby mom. So there was no fuckin' way I was ready to settle down.

But when her ass turned around and smiled that shit almost made me want to break my own rules and holla at her. Something I didn't do. I let the bitches flock to me. I never had to work for pussy and didn't plan to start that shit now. Especially for some random bitch I saw for the first time, no matter how sexy she was.

Just as I was getting back in my tinted out Altima I received a phone call from Carina my soon to be baby mama. Her ass started talking about how she heard I was at the schoolhouse. She wanted me to bring her some food and slide through her spot. I didn't mind bringing her ass something from McDonald's but that was all her ass was getting from me. She definitely wasn't wife material. Her pussy was straight and I had been fucking with her for a minute which is why I was willing to buy her ass anything at all.

After she spent what seemed like ten minutes complaining about me talking to other bitches I hung up on her ass. I really wanted to stop fucking with Carina but she was pregnant so I was stuck. The thought of us having a baby together stressed me the fuck out. It seemed like once Carina got some of this dope dick she lost her fucking mind and trapped me by getting pregnant. She knew no matter what I was a real ass nigga and would take care of mine. Which is why I couldn't just leave her ass alone. If she was carrying my seed I had to put up with her ass. I had about an hour until my meeting with the connect leaving me enough time to kick it with her for a minute.

I wasn't just some typical young nigga in the streets that hustled the block. I might fuck around and not want an old lady but shit I was only nineteen. My only focus was getting money. That's how I got my nickname.

Last year I was in high school and now I was running the damn city. I got kicked out for a weapons charge because I had some heat in my trunk. Instead of being another statistic I took classes at the community college and graduated from the adult high school with a regular diploma. I was a young boss out here working my way up, bleeding the block day in and day out. All of my hard work was finally paying off. I was getting into some real shit and was ready to start stacking my paper. So no matter what Carina or any bitch wanted, they weren't getting shit from me other than a hard dick.

When I pulled up I saw that Carina's people were gone which meant she was the only one home like usual. I knocked on the door once and she opened it fast as fuck with a mean ass mug. Even with her face twisted and the attitude she still was sexy. She was ratchet but still bad. Carina had a lot of fucked up ways but she was a down ass bitch who was loyal. I never had to worry about her creeping with another nigga even though I wasn't her nigga. Loyalty was hard to come by whether it was a nigga or a bitch. In the life I lived it meant everything.

I didn't have time for her dumb shit and really just wanted to get my dick wet as soon as possible. So I walked right past her down the hall to her room. I was a cocky ass nigga and knew she couldn't resist whatever I was willing to give. If she wanted a relationship or whatever I wasn't the nigga for her. I never made promises to her or made shit official. She knew what it was and if she didn't like it she didn't have to fuck with me at all.

Of course she followed right behind me like I knew she would. As soon as I was in the room I took off my retro Jordan's. I placed them near the bed and unbuckled my true religion jeans.

"Get on your knees and put that fucking mouth to work," I told her.

I was ready for Carina to put that mouth to work since all she wanted to do was talk shit. She looked at my now hard eleven inch dick and dropped to her knees instantly. I'm a confident nigga and I know what I'm working with and how to use my dick to please.

She opened her mouth a little at first taking just the tip in and licking all around the head like it was her favorite lollipop. Then she deep throated my shit and I felt her tonsils at the head of my dick. She began to slurp and vibrate her throat just how I liked.

I grabbed ahold of the back of her head and started moving her up and down my dick. She had tears in her eyes from the way I was handling her. But she liked that rough shit and it just made her go harder. I was trying to hold my nut so I could finish in her pussy. I told her to get up and take off all the shit she was wearing.

I watched her undress as I stroked my dick in the palm of my hand. Carina was a dark skin beautiful girl, her mentality was where she was fucked up at. She wanted nothing out of life and I couldn't see myself being with somebody who had no ambition and sat up in the house all day waiting to be fucked.

I wanted to see her pussy as I slid my dick in, so I had her get on the bed and bust it open. Carina placed both of her feet on the floor while she used her fingers to massage her clit. I grabbed both of her legs and put them over my forearms, then scooted her ass off the bed at an angle where I could be in control. I watched my whole dick slide in her pussy that was already wet and ready for me. Since getting pregnant her pussy was leaking even more than it used to. The curve in my dick always hit every woman's g spot as I put it in and I loved the look on their faces when I made them cum the first time.

As soon as I was balls deep I began beating her shit up with no mercy. Her ass cummed back to back but I wasn't done with her yet. I pulled out and turned Carina around. I wanted to watch her ass bouncing back while I fucked her. I reached around and rubbed her clit as I long stroked her from the back.

"Cum on my dick Carina. You wanted it. Take the dick. Don't run now" I said while driving her ass her crazy from the slow strokes.

"This why you been acting up? You needed me to fuck you?"

"Yes MONEY!" She screamed out.

I felt her pussy tighten around my dick again then juices flowed out even more than before. Finally, I let my nut go, then pulled out. I left her ass leaned over the bed how I had been fucking her. I usually strapped up when fucking bitches, but since Carina was already pregnant and didn't fuck around with other niggas I stopped. Shit it was too late to be worried about getting her ass pregnant and feeling the pussy raw made it that much better.

I went to the table beside her bed where I knew she kept the wet wipes and grabbed one to wipe my dick off. After cleaning myself up I continued to get dressed. I had to get up out of there so I could make it to the meeting ahead of time. I always liked to be early when I conducted business.

I knew Carina wanted to have a conversation or some shit but I wasn't there for all that. So I finished putting my jeans and shoes back on. Carina finally found her voice again. The first thing she said was some stupid shit I didn't have time for.

"Money, you know I love you and I want us to be a family when I have this baby. Are you gonna stop fuckin' around on me or what? If not just let me know so I won't wait on you anymore. I can find the next nigga to dick me down and break me off when I need it."

Was this bitch serious? We were both nineteen years old and she was talking about being a family and fucking other niggas for money in the same sentence. I didn't even bother saying anything back to her dumb ass. I finished putting on my shoes, then headed out of the room and out the front door of the house.

As soon as I closed the fuckin' door I heard what sounded like yelling coming from inside. But I didn't have time for that shit. I just wanted to get some head, fuck, and now I wanted to make some more money.

Carina was my main bitch by default. But every time I fucked her she did some shit that had me reconsidering if it was even worth the headache. I couldn't imagine being tied to her ass for life.

As I jumped in my ride the girl I saw earlier at the high school came to mind. I wish it had been her I was fucking with instead of Carina's ass. She was hands down the most beautiful girl I had ever seen. Her smile had my dick hard and her eyes had my ass in a damn trance when she turned around. Plus she surprised the hell out of me with that "have a good day" shit. No other bitch would act like she did in the same situation. They would have either flipped the fuck out, caused a big ass scene or been on me or my brother's dick trying to fuck.

It was like she didn't have a care in the world and wasn't bothered by the shit in the least. I knew she caught me staring at her ass too. I did what the fuck I wanted and made sure to let her see that shit. These bitches out here were full of drama and always trying to find a nigga like me to take care of them. But lil mama wasn't affected by me or my brother in the least. That shit made me more interested in her ass then I had been in any other bitch. Damn who was shorty?

Larissa

My day had gone from bad to worse with my last class having a pop quiz that I wasn't ready for at all. I made my way out of the front of the school and happened to see the same boy who opened his car door into mine. He was standing by the curb with one of the underclassmen hoes named Janae.

I just kept walking past ol' boy when he called out to me. So I stopped and looked in his direction. He had a smirk on his face similar to the sexy ass man he was riding with earlier. Throughout the day my mind kept wandering back to that man I laid eyes on this morning. Even in the middle of my quiz I caught myself thinking about whether he was smart or if he was a typical dumb nigga. It was obvious he was a thug by the way he dressed and his demeanor, and that only made me more intrigued with him. I had to stop thinking about the mystery man though because I probably wouldn't see his ass again.

"What's up?" I asked.

"My bad about earlier shorty I was just playin' around." He held out his hand for me to shake

"I'm Maurice please accept my apology".

His apology was almost funny but when I realized he was serious I smiled at him and shook his hand back.

"I'm sorry, I just wasn't expecting an apology. My name's Larissa and It's no big deal don't sweat it."

Of course Janae had to roll her eyes. None of these thot bitches liked me even though I never said two words to them. They were the true definition of haters anyway which I definitely wasn't gonna waste energy worrying about. I started to walk away but before I could step off the curb, the car from the morning pulled up in front of where Maurice was standing blocking my way.

I then went to walk around the back of the car to make my way over to where I was parked. I figured the man from this morning was driving again and I wanted to hurry up and get the fuck out of there before I had to see his ass again. While I was crossing over, the driver side door opened up and the man from earlier stepped out in front of my path. Today was definitely not my day.

When I stopped and looked at him I swear my heart skipped a damn beat and it was like I couldn't form a complete thought. He stood over me, but was shorter than Maurice. He had broad shoulders and a strong build. This man's sexy complexion was a rich dark chocolate color making me unintentionally smile thinking about how good he looked. He was just standing there staring at me with a smirk on his face like he knew what I was thinking, so I quickly recovered and replaced my smile with a look of indifference. He had shoulder length dreads which were pulled back out of his face making him even sexier.

This man was looking like money, but more than that he had a presence about him which emitted power and strength. I could tell he was in the streets and not like the fake ass boys running around pretending to be a thug. There wasn't a doubt in my mind that he was a real boss. I picked up on all this without even hearing him say a word while we had our eyes locked like we were sizing each other up.

I decided to speak up first since he rudely blocked my path when I was minding my own business and I wanted to know what his problem was. I never was shy.

I usually tried not to waste my time on saying things without there being a good reason.

"Can I help you?"

I asked with more attitude than I was actually feeling. He had me all in my feelings but I had to get that shit in check quick. It was hard with the intimidating man I was staring up at. He didn't even break eye contact with me while I spoke.

"Take a ride with me shorty."

I was thinking what the fuck was wrong with this nigga? I didn't even know him and his cocky ass had me out of character as it was. Then he was bold enough to ask me to get in the car with him like he was doing me a favor.

"I don't even know you, why would I get in a car with you? Plus you don't know me. That makes no sense."

"What's your name then?" he asked.

I laughed and began walking away again trying to get around him. I needed to put some space between us fast. I was tempted to reach out and touch him and see what his body felt like and I didn't even know the nigga's name. He grabbed my arm so I stopped again. His touch felt so damn good and sent chills down my spine.

"What's up?" I said quietly.

"I'm letting your fine ass know right now you're mine! I might not know your name but by the way your body responding that shit don't matter anyway ma."

"Whatever." I replied and started on my way again, "And don't bet on that shit!"

His arrogant ass really was talkin' crazy. I rushed to get in my car and closed the door as fast as possible. Before I started it up, I took a minute to relax my breathing and calm my nerves. This man, had bossed up on me and turned my whole day around with a few words. Now here I was smiling big as hell over the nigga. Damn I was in trouble if I ever saw his ass again.

Messiah (Money)

"Damn." I said while getting back in my ride.

I was stuck in a trance by this girl and the connection I felt after spending only a few minutes around her which was unexplainable. I had to have her. She was beautiful but not in the typical hoodrat or video hoe type of way. She seemed classier, like she was a queen in her own right. Although, I knew she was still in high school, she left me feeling like I needed to get her close to me as soon as possible. Which was crazy because I'm all about money and anything else or anyone else outside of family doesn't get my time or attention.

Maurice spoke up, "Her name is Larissa, I stopped lil mama earlier to apologize for being an ass this morning with the little car situation".

Her name was Larissa and I thought that shit was even sexy. It was obvious that she was mixed, she was exotic looking and that shit worked for her. She looked one of a kind and everything about her seemed perfect to me. I never was attracted to a girl like her but there was just something about her that made me want to claim her. There was no doubt in my mind that I would have Larissa and I knew I would be seeing her ass again real soon. I'm that nigga and I make shit happen.

As soon as we pulled out of the school parking lot I told him I was dropping him off at home. Even though I was deep into this street shit like my older brother and the rest of my family, I wanted Maurice to graduate from high school and then make it in life the legit way. I didn't want to constantly worry about him being knocked or something worse. I knew this game didn't love nobody. Maurice was a baller anyway. He had a bright future playing ball at somebody's college. He had so much potential and I was going to make sure he stayed out of these streets no matter what.

Me on the other hand, I was always a street nigga. I wanted not only to make a lot of money but I had a hunger for the lifestyle I was just now starting to get a taste of. My need to get this money wouldn't be satisfied and I knew this street shit was where I was meant to be. Slowly I was becoming a beast out here and nobody was going to get in the way of my goals. In the end, I was going to be running NC and hopefully the entire East Coast from Virginia to Miami.

I made my way across town into the old neighborhood where my mama still stayed. It was just her and Maurice in my childhood home now. In the city the small houses were packed close together like sardines in a can. I loved my hood and still spent most of my waking hours on the block but I refused to lay my head where I made my money.

There was too many niggas who wanted my spot and would do anything to get it. I tried to get my mama to move out of the hood too, to the suburban neighborhood across the bridge and away from all the chaos the hood brought. But she refused every time I brought it up, telling me she didn't want all those nosey white people in her business. I knew eventually she would come around because the deeper I got into this drug game there was no way I was about to let her stay here where she was a sitting duck. Plus everybody in the hood always knows everybody's business so her reasoning didn't make any damn sense.

I swerved in and out of traffic. I hated this shit more than anything else about the city. As I pulled up in front of my mama's house I saw my two right hand niggas over at the corner store. When they saw my car parked they made their way over.

I loved my Altima with the five percent tint. It cost me around $10,000 cash. It was my first purchase from my hustling profits. At this point I could afford a brand new car but to me I wasn't ready for anything flashy yet. I wanted to establish myself and my funds first. In my mind I needed to make a few moves before I felt I was at the next level with what I was trying to create. Which is why my mind was focused on the meeting I had earlier.

When they approached me, I was sure they could tell some important shit was on my mind because I still hadn't acknowledged them yet. Usually I would give a head nod even though I was a quiet nigga. But right now my mind was consumed with the deal I just made.

Earlier today when I left Carina's crib I met up with my new connect who goes by the name Fe. This nigga was from Belize and so far had been the real fucking deal when it came to hooking me up with some good shit at top rate prices.

Fe had been my connect for the past four months and I was copping a key for around twenty thousand apiece. Every other nigga across North Carolina was paying at best twenty-five, so I was making a lot more fucking profit than all them. That was the reason why I was sitting so comfortable now.

But I was hungry, shit I was starving out here according to my standards. That's why when Fe came to me with this new deal I couldn't pass the shit up. I knew it would mean more sleepless nights and more problems. But if I set the shit up right my team and me would have the whole state on lock, not just the city.

He offered to front me two hundred keys of dope with me paying him back a flat three mill before we would come to new terms on future shipments. If everything played out right with this deal I was looking at making around a two million dollar profit just on the first shipment after only two months.

This move would put my operation on the map and allow us to move into other cities across the state. Within the year we would be the only operation supplying NC. This was the type of deal niggas only dreamed of which is exactly why I was still skeptical of the whole thing.

According to Fe, his boss liked the way I worked and had been watching how I handled shit for the last year. That all sounded good to me but I wasn't a dumb nigga like a lot of mothafuckas. So I planned on making sure I lived up to my end of the agreement and would damn sure be keeping my eyes and ears open for anything out of the ordinary with this deal. The shipment was coming in two weeks from today so I had to get my team situated now.

As Draco and Silk approached my whip they each opened a door and got in. Silk sat in the passenger seat while Draco sat in the back, and slid over to the middle seat like always. These two were more like brothers to me than friends or business partners.

Silk's real name was Kenneth and he grew up with me from diaper days. Our mothers were best friends who grew up together too. He was the level headed one out of the three of us. Silk liked to take his time when making a decision and always thought shit out before a word came out of his mouth. But even though he took his time, he was a killer at heart.

I think he enjoyed taking lives more than anything else we were into. Plus the way he remained so calm and calculated when he put in work that shit wasn't normal.

He was smart as hell and graduated high school early because of it. Even though he was smart and could figure his way out of almost any problem that came his way, he couldn't escape the problems he had with the hoodrats he loved so much.

Now my nigga Draco was actually my cousin. We didn't start hanging out until we were ten and he moved up to Wilmington from Miami. Since the first day he came in my mama's house with my aunt Lisa and I beat him in a game of madden we were tight as hell. The game led to us in a knock out drag down fight right in the middle of my mama's living room, breaking shit causing us to get our asses beat. That shit really showed us we were cousins because we were both some crazy ass niggas.

Matter of fact I couldn't think of one time where the three of us didn't have each other's backs and that was why we had been successful in the drug game so far. Loyalty got us this far in a short amount of time.

A little over a year ago, the summer before my senior year of high school, I had finally talked my brother Malik into giving me some work to flip. Malik who was known in the streets as Biz already had a trap house over on the East Side where his homies lived. He was in the process of opening up another spot with the goal of taking over the city afterwards.

He fronted me an ounce of powder which I planned on having some heads whip up and then turn a profit of about $500 with each flip, paying him $1100. My plan was to spend all my extra time after school selling the shit.

So I decided to put my niggas on in hopes of getting rid of the product within a week. We ended up flipping it in a day between the three of us. Within the month I tripled the amount I was getting from Malik. To me the ceiling was the limit after that.

After I got kicked out of school for that weapons charge, I was only motivated to make more money. My brother had some snitches somewhere on his team and one of them ended up ratting him out for a reduced plea. The feds picked him up on a conspiracy and firearms charge. He took the case to trial and was sentenced to 11 years. From that point on I took over his trap and expanded across the entire city.

Now I had three spots with ten workers. I kept shit small because you couldn't trust mothafuckas out here. Even with my oldest brother currently locked down I made sure he was always straight. I never wanted to be one of those niggas that forgets their family or where they came from.

I had come a long way in a year, but this deal with my connect was on a whole other level which I was ready for. Shit I had a baby on the way and needed to set shit up for the future. This new venture would help me take over the entire state which was the next step in my plan.

"Draco, what you rollin' up back there?"

I could see he wasn't bullshitting around. Draco was wild as fuck and needed to smoke weed basically all day to keep his mind focused and calm.

"Shit, you know I got that Sour D, what you thought nigga? You smoking?"

"Hell yeah, I got some important business we need to discuss anyway."

Silk finally decided to speak now that I mentioned what was really up.

"So you met with the connect today?"

"Bruh, I'm telling you right now our lives are about to change. What I'm about to tell ya'll is some boss shit. We're gonna have to be on top of everything and stay focused. We can't have no fuck ups with this shit."

"Alright, I hear you."

Draco said after he took another long pull from the blunt he had rolled. He exhaled a cloud of smoke which had the inside of my car thick as hell with that potent smell.

"So the connect said he's willing to front us a couple hundred bricks and in two months we pay three mill back. This is a chance for us to make at least two million off top. Then when we meet to settle up, we'll discuss new terms for future shipments. This will move us from being in charge of the city to taking over the whole goddamn state. We about to be the niggas in charge of all the coke flooding the streets in Raleigh, Durham, Charlotte, you name it."

"Damn we about to be some mothafuckin' millionaires, I hear that shit. But we got to put together some teams out in each of the cities with some niggas we can trust. That ain't easy Money. You know how many snakes are gonna be waiting for us to fuck up?"

"I know and we got to be on this shit like yesterday. We each need to head out to a city, spend about a week scoping things out, and then set up one trap with no more than four workers. If we keep it small at first with the expansion we shouldn't step on any toes yet. Then over time we will set up more and more spots right under their fuckin' noses. Before the so called bosses in each city suspect a thing it will be too late. We'll have every city across the state on lock and without causing a damn war."

"I'm down Money. Shit we're ready. It's time for big moves bruh. We just gotta be ten steps ahead at all times." Silk said.

"You already know." I stated.

I knew it was risky but this life we lived was life or death. There wasn't time to be scared or no shit. We knew what we signed up for, and if you don't make big moves other niggas would make them and happily take you out in the process. It was time for a lot of changes in my life because I was coming for every fucking thing.

After smoking and finishing putting the details together for our plan to work. I drove off towards the high school again. While I was sitting up in the hood smoking and chilling with Silk and Draco, my little brother had come back out ready for me to take him back up to the schoolhouse for his basketball game.

Maurice was the starting point guard on the varsity basketball team as a sophomore. He had so much potential and was already getting recruited by NC State, Duke, and UNC. That was another reason why I wanted to keep him as far away from the street life as possible.

I pulled up in the back parking lot near the gym entrance so I didn't have to walk through the metal detectors that were always kept in the main entrance. I wasn't even allowed on school property since my weapons charge and getting kicked out. But there was no way in hell I was about to walk up in a crowded ass place without being strapped.

Even though I was only nineteen I felt like an old man compared to the youngins out there. The shit I had done and seen, high school was the last place someone like me belonged. As I made my way to the door my night got even better when I noticed Larissa standing inside the entrance to the gym. She was laughing and smiling with another beautiful girl who looked older by the way she was stacked. The pecan color skin, thick thighs and fat ass would cause any nigga to do a double take. It wasn't her that had me caught up though, or my dick jumping. That was all Larissa, the girl I claimed as my soon to be woman from earlier.

Her body and looks were perfect to me. She looked out of her element here and not because she didn't fit in but she looked like a fucking queen. I liked that Larissa did regular shit like going to a basketball game and was actually watching the game and not worried about a nigga or caught up in drama like most of the bitches that came out.

I was staring her up and down and couldn't even help it if I wanted to which I didn't. I made sure to put all my attention on her so everybody else would notice too. She was mine and nobody better try and step to her whether she knew that shit or not. Mothafuckas knew better than to go against me or show disrespect in any form. That was something I didn't tolerate.

She had me ready to drag her ass out of there and take her home so I could feel what the pussy was like. Maurice would understand why I left early.

I could even see that shit in those tight ass ripped skinny jeans she had on. They weren't too tight, but I was staring at her that hard to where I could make out her pussy print. When I finally raised my gaze up to her face I saw her looking at me with her eyebrows raised. I knew I was caught but fuck it, I told her she was going to be mine anyway. She kept those hazel eyes locked on mine as I made my way over to where she and her home girl were standing.

Larissa

"What the fuck," I instantly sputtered in a hushed tone to Shanice my one and only friend I had made since moving down here.

"What bitch? You see some problems over there we need to handle?"

Shanice was always down for a fight and since knowing her for the past few months I can definitely say she was a rider and not scary in the least. I've never been able to trust other girls because since the time I got curves and developed around sixth grade the jealousy and hate started. So instead of getting mixed up with fake friends and drama I stayed to myself.

That didn't mean dumb ass girls didn't try me every chance they got because every other week it seemed to be someone claiming something about me that I never had a clue about. So yeah, I could throw these hands if I had to even though I tried to avoid that shit. But having a real friend that I knew wasn't on no jealous shit was refreshing. Plus she could bust some heads open too and was more than ready every time.

I quickly recovered from my outburst and whispered, "You remember that man I was telling you about from earlier?"

"The fine ass nigga who claimed you on spot, girl what about him?"

"He's on his way over here now! Look at me real quick and make sure there's nothing on my face or anything."

"Stop stressing, you look good like always. And who cares anyway. You were just telling me you didn't have time for a nigga to get in the way of your goals right?"

27

Before we finished the conversation the sexy ass man was all up in my face, not smiling or nothing, just staring. He licked his top lip and then tucked his lips in while clenching his jaw. I was still staring and the intense look he was giving me back had my stomach in knots so I couldn't seem to put together any words. Shanice turned her attention back to the game and I was left to dealing with the man alone.

"LaLa, I know your ass been thinkin' about a nigga all day, and since you're gonna be mine, it's only right I tell you my name. I'm Messiah."

Before I realized it Messiah placed his hand on my lower back and led me away from Shanice and for some reason my ass followed right along like a damn puppy. He only walked a few paces outside of the gym into the hall so I was close to Shanice and wasn't too worried about leaving her alone for a minute. But the small amount of privacy seemed a little too intimate for two people who just met.

I was out here with him because I really wanted him to tell me what his deal was and why he seemed so sure that we would be a couple. His confidence was attractive but very intimidating. After a slight pause, he spoke nice and low so I was the only one who could hear his words.

"I need you to go for a ride with me. And before you say no, I promise not to touch you or try no slick shit shorty. When you're with me, I got you that's my word. Now tell your friend you will call her later, but just know I'm not taking no for an answer. I'm a nigga who gets what I want".

His lips were pressed to my ear sending chills down my entire body while his commanding voice turned me on. I must be stupid as hell because the next thing I knew my legs were walking over to Shanice and I was telling her I would call her later. She tried giving me a high five and everything that bitch was so extra but I loved her ass.

We walked out together and Messiah kept his hand placed on my lower back. I could feel the heat radiating off of him and felt comfort knowing I was with him. Every time he touched me I was drawn to him more and more. It was like I couldn't get enough of the way he made me feel. Once at his car, the same car I had seen him riding in earlier, he started the engine up and let his hand rest on my thigh. He drove off like it was normal to be in this situation with me. While I felt out of place yet still interested enough to be riding around with a damn stranger.

I had never been driven around by a man who had his own car or even gone out on a real date. All the boyfriends I had were when I was younger. I actually hadn't had a boyfriend since freshman year and here I was eighteen about to graduate in the spring. So I couldn't help but to be somewhat nervous. Still, more than anything I was excited.

Messiah hadn't said anything else to me since we had been in the car making me even more anxious. During the ride to wherever we were going he turned up the music. I could tell he had some money because his car was clean and he had a good system. I liked that he dressed well and took time on his appearance but wasn't over the top flashy.

I wasn't attracted to a nigga who had to try to be the center of attention. If a man was really all that his demeanor and the way he carried himself would make him shine, not his clothes, the jewelry he wore, or the car he drove. While we were riding Messiah was blasting some Rick Ross and we were both just vibing to the music.

The car slowed down and Messiah turned down a small dirt path hidden by overhanging trees. The area looked like it didn't belong in the middle of the city. There was grass and trees and it gave the feeling of being in the country somewhere, just the two of us far away from anything or anyone else. I spent a minute taking in my surroundings and seeing if I could figure out where we were.

"Where are we?"

"This path leads to an old cemetery nobody really knows about. I found this place by accident but it's calm as fuck. I like to come out here when I wanna clear my head or to have a moment to myself."

"I can see that. It's nice out here". I said honestly.

"So what is the deal Messiah? Why are you so interested in me? You don't know anything about me."

"I know ma and believe me I'm not even this type of nigga. I don't do shit like this. But since I saw you this morning, I can't stop thinking about you. It's like you got some kind of pull on me."

"To be real Messiah, I'm not looking for anything serious. I don't want a man at all right now. I just want to graduate, go to college, and be successful. But I'm down for having a friend because you seem like a decent guy."

I don't even know why I was considering being his friend. I had never been friends with a man I was attracted to. Everything about him was tempting but I needed to stay focused on getting the hell out of my mama's house and making something out of myself. The last thing I needed was a nigga to distract me and for me to get caught up in some shit that would end badly.

"I hear you LaLa but you gotta understand when I want something I get it. So yeah we can play this friendship getting to know each other shit, but when it's all over with I'm gonna have your ass any way I want you and you'll be begging for the dick."

His ass even grabbed his dick through his pants when he said that shit and my ass sat there gawking at it. But as soon as I saw how big his dick print was my mouth went dry and there was an instant pause in our conversation. Eventually I gathered my thoughts together again.

"Wow, I can't believe you are that cocky. But I'll give you a pass on that because I'm sure you're not used to dealing with a woman like me. From now on though, let's just see about getting to know each other. And LaLa... where did you come up with that?"

"That shit fits you ma. I like the way it rolls of my tongue." He said while looking at my pussy before looking back into my eyes.

Messiah and I ended up spending the next four hours talking while parked at that old graveyard. We talked about our childhoods, our families, even about things like our religious beliefs. After the hours talking I was feeling the man more and more. He was smart, sexy, and a thug all at the same time.

Not to mention the thought of his dick kept popping into my head. The thug side to him was something completely new to me. The entire time we spent together he was turning me on more and more with his conversation alone. When he was driving me back home I was already sad about not being around his ass.

Once he pulled in front of my house it was going on two in the morning. As I began getting out of his car he reached over and turned my head with his hand resting it against my cheek. All of the sudden he pulled me towards him and kissed me. His kiss wasn't a soft peck either. He was forceful and intense with the shit. Then his tongue was in my mouth before I knew it and his other hand was pressing against my pussy through my thong. I felt my clit throbbing, waiting to be rubbed without the material in the way.

Suddenly, I realized what the fuck I was doing and pulled away. Damn it felt so good though. Instead of saying anything I hopped out of the car and buttoned my jeans back up. How the hell he even unbuttoned them without me realizing was beyond me. It was too soon for any of that but I still felt horny and unsatisfied as I walked in the front door to my mother's house.

I rushed inside and made my way down the hall as fast as possible. I needed some relief and tonight my hand would have to do the job. I was still a virgin but had experienced plenty of kissing, touching, and oral sex with my ex. It never seemed worth it to have sex though. Then I decided to leave boys alone altogether and focus on my goals. But now, I was wondering what it would have felt like to have Messiahs strong hand make me cum instead of my own.

While I lay in bed with my legs spread wide I began to rub faster on my clit with my thumb. I brought my middle finger down to my opening and glided it in. Images of Messiah popped in my mind and I imagined his dick inside me instead of my finger. Suddenly, I cummed so hard I was shaking. I rolled over still naked and drifted off to sleep thinking about what Messiah's dick would look and feel like. I knew I was in trouble.

Messiah (Money)

Dropping LaLa off was something I didn't want to do but I knew she wasn't going for fucking me yet. She wasn't the type to lay up with a nigga she just met and I could respect her more for that. I already know by the way she jumped out of the car that she was regretting going as far as she did with me. I couldn't control myself anymore if I wanted to. Looking at her perfect face, full lips, and nice ass titties all night had finally gotten to me.

Since the minute I saw her my dick was hard as hell and I had to keep myself focused because she wasn't a girl you fucked and ducked out on after. She was worth the conversation. LaLa was the nickname I decided to give her because the shit sounded good coming out and I wanted her to feel special. If she played her cards right she could end up being my main lady. I bet her pussy was leaking right now and I could hardly wait to see what she tasted and felt like.

My dick had been ready to fuck for most of the night and I needed to handle that shit sooner rather than later. I texted this shorty named Chyna who I had been fuckin for the past month or so on the regular. Chyna was a stripper bitch, but she wasn't the type that got around like most. I always made sure to strap up when I hit. Usually I didn't fuck with strippers because they were nasty as fuck but Chyna wasn't known to fuck around. She was one of the decent girls up at Mack City that was stripping to pay her college tuition. Plus her head game was A1 and she rode my dick like a pro.

After I hit Chyna up her ass texted right back telling me to meet her at the club so she could leave with me when she finished her last set. I was already on the East Side of town so I made my way to Mack's. When I pulled into the lot I noticed Silk's car over near the entrance. He drove a brand new all black Audi with tinted windows and black rims. It was a smooth ass whip. Maybe I would get one for my next car to celebrate the deal I had just made.

I parked next to Silk's ride then got out. As I stood up I made sure my shit still looked fresh. Brushing myself off, I went to my trunk next. I pulled my Ruger out and tucked it under my shirt in the back of my pants. I never left home without some heat. You could never be too careful out here. I kept a Glock in a secret compartment under the steering wheel in case some shit popped off and I didn't have time to get into the trunk.

I went right up to the doorman and walked past him with a head nod. Mack City was owned by one of my brother's homies from way back who went legit a few years ago. I never had to worry about being searched or no shit like that when I came here. Which is why I always made sure to spend plenty of money each time I visited. I hated a nigga that acted all stingy when there was no reason for it, especially when someone looked out for you.

I walked over to our usual VIP spot and saw Draco and Silk. Each of them had a stripper posted on their lap giving them a dance. One was a dark skinned slim thick bitch who didn't have any titties, but her ass was fat for her small frame. She was definitely Draco's type. I always thought those skinny bitches were a little off in the head. Plus I didn't think they had enough meat on their bones to take all the dick I had to give. Don't get me wrong though I had come across a few who knew how to handle shit just fine too. I would still fuck from time to time but they just weren't my type.

I had seen the bitch dancing on Silk plenty of times because she was always around Chyna. I didn't know her name or anything though. She was bent over twerking all over my nigga. When she noticed me enter the section she began making her ass pop even more while staring at me like she wanted to fuck. Shorty was bad I'm not gonna lie. She had a flat stomach, nice plump ass, a cute face and some long braids I could grab while hitting it from the back. But I didn't fuck with these strippers like that. Chyna was the exception and I didn't plan on changing shit up anytime soon. Silk slapped her ass and grabbed a handful of both cheeks before she turned around and whispered something in his ear.

I saw a bottle of Henny sitting on the table already so I poured myself a shot, threw that back and poured another. There was some stripper on stage butt naked at the top of the pole twirling around. She dropped down into a full split before going into a handstand with her pussy out and ass moving to the beat.

I spotted Chyna walking out from the back. She hurried up to get over to me and told me she was ready to go. Chyna always tried to act possessive of me every time I was here like she didn't like me to look at the other bitches. But she wasn't my bitch and I would never wife a stripper. She could catch my nut though.

I dapped my homies up, made sure they were good and left with Chyna leading the way pulling me by the hand. I didn't like a woman to be in control especially if I wasn't even claiming her, but she would remember that shit when I had her naked and face down later.

I didn't take any female to my house so I booked a room at the Holiday Inn Express. I also didn't spend money when it wasn't' necessary. The Holiday Inn was good enough for Chyna. It was clean and had decent rooms, but nothing over the top.

We made our way to the elevator and as soon as the door was closed Chyna had her hand in my pants massaging my dick. I loved public shit like this. But I liked it more when I took the lead. When the doors opened to the third floor I pulled her hand out of my pants and led the way down the hall to our room.

When we got inside, I took off my clothes. By the time I was done Chyna was on the bed naked with her ass facing me holding the perfect arch in her back. I could see her fat pussy glistening from between her legs. Shit, she was already wet and ready for me. I loved to eat pussy but there wasn't no way I was putting my mouth on a stripper.

So I got on the bed behind her rolled on the condom and without warning stuck my dick all the way in her pussy. I felt her walls tighten and then adjust. She screamed out from the impact of my dick stretching her wide and hitting her spot. I hated not feeling all the sensations but her pussy was good enough to do the job and she was squeezing down on my shit. I kept digging in her guts while her ass was yelling loud as fuck.

"Yes Money, fuck this pussy, fuck your pussy."

She kept telling me to fuck her pussy, so I went harder. I grabbed her hips pulling her down even farther on my dick. Her ass was jiggling with each movement because it was so big. I slapped it hard as hell which had her going wild and bucking back more and more. I felt her juices running down my balls and knew she had cum.

I pushed her head down on the mattress and grabbed her weave making sure she felt that shit too.

"Don't fucking move Chyna. Who's the mothafuckin' boss?"

"You are daddy"

"Now keep that arch and you bet not move a fucking inch."

I began stroking her slow and deep making sure she did what the fuck I said. I knew she couldn't handle how deep I was going but that's what her ass gets for trying to be in control of a nigga like me. She shook and then I felt her ass was cumming again. After that she was barely able to move while I was fucking. I wasn't through with her ass yet though.

"Get up and touch your toes where I can see that shit in the mirror."

She got off the bed and spread her legs bending over so her hands were on the floor with her legs straight. I held her hips in place and rammed my dick in her as I held her up.

"Shit Money, I can't take it, Oh my GOD!"

This time I could see everything in the mirror, and wanted her to see who the fuck was in charge.

"Look up Chyna. You wanted me to fuck you, now watch this shit, I wanna see you take all the dick."

All you could hear was a slapping noise because we were both turned on and in our zone. I bet LaLa would like this shit too, she just don't know it yet I thought to myself. I felt Chyna's body tense up before her pussy started clenching my dick. I knew she was about to cum again so I gave her another long stroke. Her body almost went limp in my arms from fuckin' her right.

I pulled back out and sat on the edge of the bed. I picked Chyna up and let her slide down my dick in one motion. She turned around reverse cowgirl with me still inside and was bouncing up and down taking my full dick in each time she came down.

Her ass bouncing while I gripped it which had my nut rising. I saw her cum again this time squirting with juices coming down on my thighs. The sight had me ready to nut, so I pushed her off of me and stood up. I turned around to where she was now straddled on the bed facing me. I threw the condom across the room and put my dick in her mouth.

She knew exactly what to do. She slurped and moved up and down my shaft taking me as deep as her throat would allow. When I was about to cum I pulled out and let my seeds shoot out on her mouth dripping down her titties.

After fucking Chyna I wanted to get cleaned up and get the fuck on. I was ready to get a few hours of sleep before I started really putting in work tomorrow getting things in motion for the deal. Chyna went into the bathroom and then walked back over to me as I laid across the bed with a warm wet washcloth. She wiped my dick down. I sat up after she was done and began to get dressed. I said a few words and was on my way.

The good thing about Chyna was I never had to worry about her running her mouth and saying some dumb shit like Carina. I still couldn't believe Carina's ass was pregnant. I wasn't ready for a baby especially one with her. Shit, she wasn't wife material and definitely not mother material. What the fuck had I got myself into?

As I made my way down to my car I sent a text to LaLa. Hopefully once I got a sample of her pussy I wouldn't be caught up thinking about her all the time. I wasn't used to this shit at all. It was the first time I had thought about another woman while fucking another bitch.

Larissa

I woke up and rolled over in my bed. When I saw that it was already going on ten o'clock in the morning I knew it was time for me to get my ass up out of bed and start my day. I pulled the covers back off of me and sat up. Then I picked up my phone which was on the bedside table. I saw that I had an unread text message. I opened it up after unlocking my phone screen and saw it was from Messiah. I forgot I had given him my number before he dropped me off last night. The text was simple and said,

"Good morning beautiful just thinking of you. Hit me up when you wake up."

I saw that message was sent around four in the morning and was left wondering what he was doing after he dropped me off. I knew he was in the streets and probably sold drugs so there was no telling. The text did have me smiling like a little kid and I had butterflies in my stomach just thinking about the time we spent together last night, especially how we had left each other.

I went to my bathroom which was adjoined to my bedroom. I loved having privacy and it was probably the highlight of my move down to NC so far. That and meeting Shanice.

Back home in Illinois, I had to share a bathroom with my four step brothers and sisters. Life hadn't always been that way for me. My older brother and sister and I grew up with our single father from the time I was five until 13.

Then he decided to marry my evil ass stepmother. For real, her and her kids had something wrong with them. They made it their life mission to make my life a living hell. I got my first taste of how horrible things were going to get when my step sister snitched on me back in eighth grade.

When I arrived back home from the first middle school party I had ever gone to, where I happened to smoke weed for the first time, my dad came downstairs to my room and basically kicked the door in. He started yelling at me saying I was irresponsible and he wasn't going to have his daughter acting like a hoe. Apparently my step sister who was the same age as me was at the party and couldn't wait to get home to rat me out.

From that point on things only got worse. The people I was living with had it out for me and were some haters. Every chance they got they were lying on me or treating me like something was wrong with me. It didn't help that my father had remarried a black woman who couldn't stand the fact he had mixed children.

My sister and brother were older and already living on their own so I was the only one who had to deal with her bullshit. It was like all her insecurities made her treat me worse. Shit, it left me thinking something was wrong with me, until I finally just said fuck it and decided to move down south to live with my mother.

The thing that hurt the worst was before my father remarried I was a daddy's girl. I was the youngest and he always spoiled me with attention and time. Once he turned his back on me I turned cold to this world for the most part. I still had my grandma back home who was my escape when I needed it. But both of my parents had basically chose other people or things over their own flesh and blood.

So I definitely had some trust issues. If your own parents will do you dirty who knows what people you aren't related to will do. I still had my sister, brother, and grandma. But my parents fucked up my attitude for anyone else.

I looked at my reflection in the mirror inside the bathroom. My golden complexion, full breasts, and wide hips had my body looking like a goddess. I had a flat toned stomach with toned thighs, so you could tell I was athletic. But my hourglass shape and round ass made men drool when I walked by. I had a pretty bald pussy that sat up nice. I admired my body for another minute and thought about how bitches paid to look like I did and mine was all natural. I knew whoever I decided to give my virginity to would be a lucky man. Any man who had me on their arm was lucky enough. I wasn't conceited but I did appreciate my beauty and self-worth.

Before picking out my clothes, I needed to figure out something to do to get out of this house. It was a bright sunny morning already and since it was late March it was probably going to be around seventy degrees. I dialed up Shanice to see if she had anything planned.

"Good morning friend, what are your plans for today?"

"Nothing bitch, but you remember that fine ass man I been telling you about? The one I been trying to swerve and he keeps steady calling? She asked.

"Yeah I remember the big sexy ass nigga that you keep telling me about."

Shanice had been out in the hood at her cousin's house about two weeks ago and some tall light skin mystery man approached her. Somehow she had given in and he got her number. He had been trying to take her out since. She kept flirting with him through texts and when they talked over the phone but never would let him take her anywhere. She swore up and down he was

42

a no good nigga and a hoe around town but I could tell she was feeling him.

"Well bitch he wants me to go to some club by the pier tonight. It's supposed to be a grown and sexy crowd so no problems. But you know I only agreed if I could bring a friend. Shit he finally broke a bitch down and got me to meet up with him. So you're coming right?"

"Neesy you know the whole partying and club scene ain't me girl. I got to stay focused to get the fuck up outa here in the next couple months as soon as graduation happens."

"I know girl but how much harm can one night do? Plus I really need my best friend for this one. I don't want that sexy ass man to convince me of some shit I'm a regret later.

"Fine. But you know I ain't got nothing to wear and what time is it at?"

"You're the best LaLa. You know I got you. I'll come scoop you up around noon. We can grab lunch then stop by the mall to get something to wear. Don't worry about paying me back either."

"Alright. And why you call me LaLa, what's with everybody changing my name?

"I heard your man use it last night for your information and figured since you're all in love now that was what you was going by." Shanice said as she began laughing.

"Whatever. I'll see you in a few."

I hung up the phone and made my way over to my closet to pick out my clothes for the day. I chose a yellow strapless maxi dress and some tan gladiator wedges to go with it. I wanted to be cute since we were going to the mall but still comfortable. I loved sun dresses and this weather was perfect for them. I also chose a canary yellow thong to wear and decided against wearing a bra. My breasts would sit up well with the support the dress gave.

After setting the clothes on my bed, I went to start the shower up. I turned the hot and cold water on to where the water was hot enough to form steam. Then I stepped in and the water immediately had me feeling refreshed. I shaved my legs, my underarms, and my pussy. Even though I waxed I liked to keep my skin as smooth as possible all over. I let my hair down from the messy bun I had it in and washed it. To finish off, I picked up my loofa and lathered up some of the mango body wash that I loved. I rubbed my entire body down, then rinsed off. After turning off the water, I stepped out and dried off.

I wrapped the towel around my body so I could moisturize and blow dry my hair. I was going to keep my curls like I did most days. Even with my hair dried it still reached the middle of my back. I dropped the towel in the hamper that was near the door and rubbed my favorite coconut oil all over my body. I left out of the bathroom and went over to my bed where I slipped my panties on, then the dress over my head. Next I stepped into my wedges and buckled them. I added a few gold bangles and gold hoop earrings to finish the outfit. I sat on my bed with my compact and eyeliner to finish getting ready.

As soon as I was done, I picked my phone up and started scrolling through my newsfeed. I saw a few of the people I went to school with had gone to a party last night, but otherwise nothing was catching my attention. I opened my messages back up to the one Messiah had sent. I wasn't planning on communicating with him anymore to be honest. I was scared of falling for him which I could see happening after the time we spent together last night. I figured it was only a matter of time before he fucked me over. But I decided that texting and just being friends wouldn't hurt. I typed a quick message.

"Thanks for the text. I enjoyed last night. Have a good day," hitting the send button before I could change my mind.

I saw that he had messaged me back almost immediately.

"Hey ma what took you so long to hit me up? I know you was thinking about me since last night. I wanna see you later."

I read the message and was smiling the whole time again.

"Sorry, but I got plans today. I'll get up with you another time."

It seemed like as soon as I sent the message my phone started vibrating with a call from none other than Messiah. What the hell was his crazy ass calling me for when we just were texting?

"Hello, what's up Messiah?"

"Cut the shit LaLa I'm not with waiting for you to decide when you're gonna make time for me. I wanna see your ass today, but since you got plans already I'll give you a pass. But tomorrow morning I'm picking your ass up at ten so be ready."

"Whatever, nigga you don't run me. I'll see what I can do and let you know tomorrow." I said back to his overbearing ass.

"Play with me if you want to girl, but don't say I didn't warn you. Now tell me you missed me and then I'll let you get ready for whatever plans you got."

"I'm not admitting to anything Messiah, you are too damn cocky."

"Oh yeah, I bet your panties wet as fuck just from hearing my voice."

"Boy bye, I'll talk to you later."

I was laughing it off to him but the truth was I had been thinking about him from the time I went to sleep and since I woke up.

I went ahead and put my phone into my purse since I knew Shanice would be by soon. The last thing I wanted was for her to have to wait on me and actually come in the house. Not that there was anything wrong with where I lived, except for my racist ass step-father. He wouldn't say any slick shit when my mama was home but whenever she was gone to work at the hospital he would try me.

Last weekend he made some comment about how I should take a shower since my skin still looked dirty trying to be funny. He then went on to say I had nigger lips and they were too big to be drinking out of his cups. That was the type of shit he was always doing especially on the weekends when my mom had to work until the afternoon. Not to mention the way he looked at me just didn't sit right with me either. It was like he stared at me with disgust and desire at the same time. He just creeped me out.

So on the weekends I basically stayed in my room or tried to find a way to get out of the house until I knew my mother would be home. I brought up the subject of her racist ass husband one time and she laughed it off like what he said wasn't really that bad. When she did that I knew I had to forget about any real relationship with her and just focus on getting the hell up out of here as soon as possible. I didn't understand how my parents were more worried about their spouses than their own child.

Just as I looked back at the clock to check the time, I heard a car horn sound which let me know Neesy was outside. I scooted off the bed and hurried my ass up through the hall to the front door. I saw my step dad out of the corner of my eye sitting in the living room but avoided looking his way. I came down the porch steps ready to grab some food and chill out with my best friend.

Shanice came from a really good family that had plenty of money so when we went out together she usually would drive. Her parents bought her an all-white Jeep last spring for keeping her grades up. Me and her were a lot alike when it came to doing well in school. We weren't your average cute dumb girls that couldn't hold a conversation. We both maintained high GPA's and took school seriously.

We both had problems but kept our goals our priority. That was one of the reasons we clicked so well. Shanice didn't live anywhere near the hood. She actually stayed in a rich ass neighborhood full of historic houses. There was even a country club. She had always attended public school and had cousins who lived on the Southside and Eastside. Every chance she got she was in the hood doing some crazy shit. She wasn't a hoe that slept around or anything, she just liked to be with "her people" as she always said.

She never judged anyone based on what they looked like, how much money they had, or where they came from. I appreciated that most about her because for once I wasn't judged for not being black enough or for not being white.

I grew up at the bottom of the barrel poor but had lived in rented out houses in middle class neighborhoods. Both my parents wanted to stay out of the hood so bad. While Shanice was born with a silver spoon in her mouth and never wanted for shit, she only wanted to spend time in the hood. It's funny how life goes sometimes.

Shanice knew all kinds of things I had never even heard of. She knew who the thugs were, what the gossip was around town, and everything else. While I had only been to the hood when Shanice and me rode through. I didn't know anything about the street life, which is another reason I was worried about spending more time with Messiah.

I didn't know what his life entailed or how I could possibly fit into his world. The shit he was probably into I had no clue about. I definitely didn't want to get caught up in anything illegal and risk my future plans. I would just have to take it day by day and hope for a friendship with him at best anyway.

Shanice

I was more than ready to pick up my best bitch and go find some new outfits for this party tonight. This nigga I ran into a couple weeks back had been texting and calling me since the day we met. I still remember the first time I laid eyes on him. He was a light skin nigga just the way I like them. He had a nice trimmed beard, a tapered fade, grey eyes, and some pink lips. He was sexy as hell to me. I was only around five feet six inches and he had to be around six feet tall with a body that was nothing but muscle. He had on all black from his Timbs up to his fitted hat. Both of his arms were full of tattoos from what I could see. The thing I liked most about him was how he carried himself.

That nigga walked right up to where I was standing with my cousin like he was in charge of some shit. I usually came out to her side of town to chill with her after school and always would smoke one and pass the time talking about all the latest drama. I had on some high waist acid washed jeans, with a white bodysuit underneath. I was wearing a pair of wheat colored Timbs with my hair in a high bun. I was without a doubt the baddest bitch on the block and every time a nigga passed he tried to holla while I would ignore their ass.

I wasn't stuck up or no shit, I just didn't like to fuck with a lot of dudes and I was very selective with the company I kept. My ex-boyfriend had cheated on me and left me with a fuck all niggas attitude. Maybe one day I would love again but for now I just wanted to enjoy life and live it up with my friends.

So as I was talking minding my own business here comes this arrogant man who walked up out of nowhere.

But instead of saying anything to me he just stood real close to me from behind. He was close enough that I could smell his Tom Ford cologne and feel his body heat. That's how close the mothafucka was to me. I even felt his breath on my neck while I was waiting for him to stop being a weird ass nigga and say something. I still hadn't really gotten a good look at him.

Finally he cleared his throat like he was waiting for me or something. So I turned around rolling my neck in the process ready to give the ignorant nigga an earful for his disrespectful manners. As soon as I turned around I was struck silent and couldn't say a damn word. Instead he decided to speak.

"Aye girl I been watching you for a minute and I like what I see. Matter of fact what's your name and number so we can make shit happen?"

I finally found my voice. "I'm Shanice and I'm gonna have to pass on that."

"Look I know you not the type to give a nigga the time of day with your stuck up ass but that's because you ain't fucked with a real nigga yet. I'm not taking no for an answer. Here's my phone. Plug your number in and like I said we gonna make shit happen."

He said all that as a command while looking right into my eyes not breaking eye contact. It was like he was daring me to go against the shit he just spit to me. I figured why the hell not. It wasn't like I was going to answer if he called so what would be the big deal and it felt good to have a fine ass nigga like him sweating me.

I shrugged then grabbed his phone without another word and typed my digits in. We didn't exchange another word. He put his phone back in his pocket and walked away like nothing even happened. Which left me wondering what the hell his deal was. But I had to admit

50

that nigga was smooth because now here I was two weeks later getting ready to meet up with him tonight.

How he talked me into this shit I didn't know either. Actually, he probably could talk me into a whole lot of other shit too. That's why I made sure to only agree to meet up at this club if I could bring Larissa along. I knew she would look out for me and not let me get into anything I would regret later.

I also couldn't wait to hear all about that mystery nigga she left with in the middle of the game last night. Larissa had become my best friend over the past few months. I had some cousins that I was pretty tight with but they had already dropped out or graduated a couple years ago.

So whenever I was at school I stayed to myself for the most part. Everybody was on some hating ass shit or dumb shit. Now me, I just liked to do what I had to do during the school day. I didn't really like school but knew later in life it would be important to have an education. So I thought of it more like my job. It was something that needed to be done to get where I wanted later on because I wasn't trying to depend on my parent's money or some nigga to take care of me.

I felt most comfortable in the hood with my people. I wasn't a hoe out here or nothing like that. I just was a down ass chick. I felt a bond to my family from an early age and since most of them lived in the hood, that's where I wanted to be too.

None of the things that went on out here were new to me. I had been around the drug game for a long time since my cousins were deep into it. They kept me away from most of the shit they were into but made sure I knew how to handle myself. Even though my parents hated the lifestyle choices I made they stayed off my back as long as I kept my grades up and didn't get into any trouble.

My mother was a doctor at the hospital and my father was a big time lawyer in the area. We lived in an upscale neighborhood. But none of that shit appealed to me. It just wasn't me.

I first met Larissa in chemistry class last semester when she sat next to me. I sat up front in all my classes so I could pay attention. When she sat down I was somewhat surprised since there was a few extra seats at the tables in the back of the room. Most of these girls, especially pretty ones, didn't care nothing about what they were supposed to be learning in class. They were usually more worried about some lame ass high school drama or finding a come up.

We ended up clicking right away and were inseparable ever since. She was beautiful inside and out but had some trust issues. We already beat plenty of bitches asses together and told each other all of our secrets. She had become more like a sister to me than just a friend even though we hadn't known each other that long.

I pulled into Larissa's driveway and honked the horn. She came down the steps looking like a model. I realized that we both were wearing yellow and had to laugh because we always seemed to do that shit. We would pick out coordinating outfits all the time without planning it. I guess we both just had good taste. She opened the door and when she got in I could tell she had some shit to tell me.

"Spill the tea bitch. I know you got some things you want to tell me. Start with your new beau you spent the evening with last night."

I wanted to hear the details. Larissa never gave anybody a chance because she believed most people would end up hurting her like her parents had.

"I mean there's not much to tell. Messiah really surprised me last night but he seems too good to be true. He's so fine and he says he wants to get to know me. Girl he keeps saying I'm his woman, like what nigga does that the first day they meet someone."

She let out all in one breath. I could tell she was really feeling the nigga. I felt like it was past time she put her heart out there and gave somebody a chance. Hearing her say his name was Messiah caught me off guard. I had heard of a Messiah known as Money in the streets.

He was basically the nigga in charge of the whole city's drug flow. My cousins even worked under him and said he was smart as shit. The word on the street was he was young but had shit on lock and was going places. He wasn't a nigga you wanted to piss off either from what I had heard. I decided to give it to her straight, she was my girl after all.

"Look, I'm only saying this because you need to hear it. You keep trying to push away anyone who might hurt you and you not really living in the process. You gotta take chances sometimes. That doesn't mean trust every nigga. It just means sometimes there are people who you will be able to count on through thick and thin. You never know girl, just look and me and you." I said with a smile.

I knew she had fucked up parents and she felt alone in the world. But I would always have her back. She deserved to find a man who would love and cherish her even if it wasn't Messiah. She sat there in silence digesting everything I had told her. After a few minutes she continued with the conversation.

"We talked about everything last night too Neesy. He is so sexy to me. He has an effect on me that no man has ever had. I'm scared though. He's a real ass thug, which I like but I don't know shit about the streets girl. I don't want to get hurt." Larissa shared with a worried expression on her face.

"Just see where it goes, don't stress anything yet. You like him so get to know him and things will fall into place the way they're supposed to. Stop worrying and enjoy that fine ass nigga!" I encouraged her.

I decided to leave out the details of how into the streets he really was or the fact he ran city. I believed in fate and thought that if something was meant to be it would happen no matter what. I also didn't want to scare her away from him before she even gave him a chance.

"He is fine huh!" she chuckled.

Now here she was looking happy as hell all of the sudden and I knew that for now Messiah at least had a chance. He just better not fuck up and hurt her or he would have some problems with me.

We turned into the parking lot of the mall. I figured we could eat something out of the food court since I was craving Chinese anyway. Larissa was cool with whatever like usual. We stopped and ate first since we were both starving then made our way over to the stores.

I already found what I was wearing tonight. It was a tight burgundy Bodycon dress that stopped mid-thigh. I had some nude knee high boots that would go perfect with the dress. Larissa was trying on a dress that I picked out for her to wear. I knew it would fit her perfect.

All I was told about tonight was that it was a grown and sexy party being thrown at this club downtown. I had heard of the club but never been. It was known for hosting different events and was usually a by invite only place to attend.

Larissa came out of the dressing room, and I sat back to take in the sight of her. She looked amazing in the dress. She was already a beautiful girl but the dress had her looking like a sexy ass grown woman. It had her full curves on display and showed off her ass and breasts which were usually hidden underneath her regular clothes.

Larissa always dressed nice but modest so this dress was something completely new to her. It was a black off the shoulder form fitting dress that stopped just under her ass, making it cuff at the bottom. She had on a pair of Valentino black pumps to match. Yes my bitch was certified and tonight we would be walking in killing all the hoes up in the club without a doubt.

Thinking about tonight reminded me that I would have to see the man I had been trying to steer clear of too. Damn we both had some niggas getting our heads all fucked up but hopefully it would be worth it.

Larissa

As I looked at myself in the full length mirror I hardly recognized my own reflection. Usually I looked good, but this dress had me looking like a grown ass woman that was famous or something. I was starting to get excited about going out tonight because it was something I had never experienced.

Through the mirror I saw a group of men enter the store. There was three of them and while two went over to the men's section the best looking one stopped and made his way in my direction. He was wearing a suit but he had an edge to him that made him attractive. He didn't seem like he was a suit and tie type of nigga in the first place but he pulled it off well.

As he approached I realized he had dreads like Messiah but was lighter skinned and a little taller. He came up behind me while I was still tying on the dress. He was looking me up and down and said in a deep tone,

"I had to come over here. You're the most beautiful woman I've ever seen. That dress fits you perfect. You got a man?"

I smiled politely and turned around.

"No I don't have a man but I'm not looking for one right now. Thanks for the compliment."

He kept watching me to gauge my reaction and eventually shook his head as he spoke his next words.

"Alright ma, but when you do start looking make sure you get up with me."

He handed me his business card and walked away to join up with the rest of his boys. He was really attractive and handled himself well but he didn't put butterflies in my stomach like Messiah did. I turned the card over in my hand and read it over. His name was Shamar and he was into real estate. Maybe one day I would find a use for the card or decide to take him up on his offer. I walked back into the dressing room and changed back into the sundress I wore in. Then placed the card in my billfold before stuffing it in my purse.

Shanice bought the dress and told me not to worry about it since it was on her parent's black card anyway. We left out of the mall and decided to head over to Shanice's house to relax before getting ready for the night.

Messiah (Money)

So far the day had gone exactly as I had planned. Silk, Draco, and I were all at our warehouse. The property was located around 50 miles north of the city. Whenever we were discussing business we did that shit in person to avoid getting caught up by twelve. Only the three of us knew about this location.

We also had a house we rented downtown to discuss business with our crew that ran the three traps across town. There was levels to our operation so that if some shit went down and there was a snake on our team we could keep the damage to a minimum. The only people who knew the ins and outs of our entire operation were the three of us and that was how we were gonna keep shit no matter how big we got.

I was the boss technically which happened naturally since I put Silk and Draco on when we first started hustling. At this point I was the only nigga that had met our connect. I trusted my partners enough to meet him but he only wanted to deal with me right now since our partnership was still new. We already made our flights for the following day to head out to each of the main cities in the state. It was important we get the ball rolling on our plans.

I called a meeting earlier with our crews in town at the house we kept. They were instructed to keep shit moving the same way it usually did while we were gone out of town. The only difference from how we normally ran shit was going to be us letting each of the lieutenants take the money and perform the drop off without one of us being present.

This was a leap of faith for us but if we were going to move to the next level and create the organization I had in mind it was necessary. Each crew had their own stash spot to get product from and another spot where there were safes for the money. We never kept our product and money where business was conducted or at the same location. That way if we got hit by the police or another crew our loss would be less.

The network we already had set up allowed us to all stack around a half million so far. We were in the process of getting businesses up and running to clean the money and I recently hired an accountant. This was only the beginning of our enterprise that would make all our drug money become legal money. This deal had come at exactly the right time because we needed more revenue to make shit happen the right way.

Our warehouse was on a ten acre plot of land surrounded by woods. It took about an hour to get there from the city but the drive was well worth not taking the risk of making certain moves under watchful eyes. We met up here once a week to go over the logistics of our operation. We also had a spot in the back to handle any mothafuckas that needed to be dealt with. I kept my pit bulls that I bred on the property too.

They were some big ass reds and blues that I took a lot of pride in. I trained them personally from pups to be deadly so we didn't have to worry about trespassers fuckin' with our shit. I had a state of the art kennel set up for them. I always kept two loose between the boundary fences in case some dumb ass decided not to follow the warning signs we had posted along the road that read "No Trespassing". You could never be too careful about anything, and I wasn't trying to get locked up before I really even got started.

We were wrapping up the conversation and just kicking it while we sat around the cherry oak table that was in the middle of the main room. It felt good to be the boss nigga of my city and I couldn't wait until we were running the whole damn state. Tonight we were meeting up with some of the city's top black business owners who had started off in the streets and turned legit over the years. The event was being held at a club downtown. We were invited by my nigga Mack who owned the strip club. I guess he gave the invite to Draco and Silk last night way before I came through and picked up Chyna's ass.

I wondered what Larissa had planned tonight that she couldn't see me. She better not be out with no other nigga I thought to myself as I finished the blunt I was smoking. I knew better though. She seemed liked a good girl and barely wanted to give my ass a chance.

I stood to leave, dapped my boys up and decided to head home. It was around dinnertime so I could run to my house and grab something to eat on the way. I planned to meet up with Silk and Draco later at the club. I opened the door to my brand new Audi A7 that I purchased earlier and made my way south. It was time to celebrate this deal because tomorrow we would be putting in work beginning to stake claims on new territory.

Carina

I was sitting at home like usual watching my shows when my little sister Janae walked in. She spotted me on the couch and sat down beside me. Janae was a cute girl and we looked so much alike that we could even pass for twins. We were only a year apart and best friends. There wasn't shit I wouldn't do for my little sister.

I lived with my mama for the time being but once the baby I was carrying was born I would be out of here. I hated living here. My mother was one of those over the top Christian frauds who spent every waking moment in church. The problem was she forgot about her two kids at home. She had been addicted to crack all my life until five years ago when she found Jesus.

I was glad she was off the dope, but she just traded one addiction for the next. She didn't look out for me or Janae and so we were stuck out here doing what we had to in order to survive. I was fourteen years old when I sucked my first dick for cash. I had to get it by any means so me and my little sister had food to eat. At least when my mama was a dope fiend she went out and stole us some shit to eat. Once she was saved it was like we didn't exist at all.

I had been turning tricks for money for years but kept it on the low. I only had a few clients that I dealt with. I wasn't fucking with any and everybody and only had sex with four men. Three of them being the niggas I tricked off on and the other one being Money.

The men I had in rotation were over twice my age so no one ever found out what I was up to. Janae knew what I did to support us because I would let them come over here since our mother was always gone.

I was happy as hell that I had gotten pregnant by Money. That nigga was gonna take care of me for life since I would be the mother of his child. Me and him met freshman year of high school and started fucking every chance we got soon after. He always used condoms for the first few years. But over the last year, I caught his ass a few times when he had too much to drink or came over high out of his mind.

I knew how he liked for me to deep throat his dick and hum on the tip. That shit always made him putty in my hands. As soon as he tensed up I would move fast as hell to get on top of him before he could stop me. I'd put my pussy to work on his ass and I would squeeze my muscles as I slid up and down without stopping just to make sure I could catch all his nut. Then afterwards I made sure to lay down without getting up to keep all of his cum in me longer.

The few times I fucked him without a condom paid off. After the fifth time I got the best news of my life and was expecting my first child with not only the nigga I loved, but the man who was my ticket out of this fucked up life I was living. Call me what you want but at the end of the day I was going to do whatever it took to survive out here.

I knew Money had other bitches he was fucking with and I really didn't care since I was doing my own dirt. As long as he took care of me and the baby and broke me off with that big ass dick when I needed it, I had no problems playing my role as his number one.

Whenever he stopped paying attention to me or I heard about him being seen with another bitch I went crazy on his ass. I would call him back to back, show up in the hood at the spots I knew he would be at and make a big ass scene.

I always let him know that he had to treat me right since I was with him from the beginning. True we never made it official but I was patiently waiting. He would come around in time and make me wifey when he was ready. In the meantime I had to make sure he didn't give no other bitch too much of his attention or he found out about what I was up to on the side.

I still had niggas on the side because they were supporting me. The one thing about Money was he didn't just give handouts because he was fucking you. We usually didn't go out together anywhere. The few times we had been to restaurants they were always drive through spots and he would pay. He wasn't into letting me hold shit either and never took me shopping or no shit like that. But with the baby on the way he already told me I didn't have to worry about anything.

As we were sitting on the couch Janae's phone rang. She picked it up and started having a loud ass conversation. I rolled my eyes as she walked out of the room sticking her tongue out at me. I wondered who her new flavor of the week was. Janae was like me, the only difference was she let her shit be known. She was considered a hoe around town and had no shame about trying to make these niggas come out of their pockets for fucking her.

Larissa

We ended up falling asleep when we got back to Shanice's house. Her home was absolutely beautiful and I loved coming over. It was so relaxing over here and most of the time her parents were working so they were rarely home. They called and checked in with her regularly though which let me know that they truly cared about her even though they weren't around much.

When we woke up it was already past ten and time for us to start getting ready for our night out. The more Shanice talked about how turnt we were about to be tonight the more hyped I got. This was the first time I had been to a club in my life. I turned eighteen last October but never felt the need to check out the whole club scene.

When Shanice gave me that advice earlier it made me realize I was missing out on more than just experiencing a real relationship with a nigga. I was also missing out on living life. I always kept my guard up so that nobody would hurt me again which caused me to miss out on so many opportunities like going to parties, having fun, and being a typical eighteen year old.

So it felt good to be opening up somewhat. I decided that I was going to take more chances. Tonight I planned on going all out and wanted to turn the fuck up. Couldn't nobody tell me nothing with the way I was looking and feeling.

It only took us an hour to get primped and ready to head out, so we opted to take a couple of shots before leaving and smoke a blunt. I wasn't a heavy drinker or smoker but I wasn't new to the shit either. We wanted to loosen up but not overdo it since we really didn't know much about the atmosphere of the club we were heading to. Shanice rolled up because out of the two of us she was damn near a pot head.

We sat back passing the blunt until we started to feel the effects of the alcohol and weed. We grabbed our purses and both took one last look in the mirror to make sure we looked good before heading out. The club was across town and was only a ten minute drive normally. But the way we were cruising it was more like five.

Shanice had her music turned all the way up and we were dancing and singing along to Kevin Gates. Near downtown we ended up at a stoplight with some white men next to us in a clean ass Mercedes. I was feeling myself from the drinks so I looked over and blew them a kiss and waved. The men rolled down their window and started whistling and trying to get our attention more. Shanice sped off fast as hell as soon as the light turned green. She started talking shit while I was laughing hard as hell.

"What the hell you do that for bitch! You trying to get us killed by some white men out here?"

She was trying to sound mad but I could tell she thought that shit was funny too.

"Bitch you know I was just playing. Have some fun girl, tonight is your night anyway. I know you're ready to see that nigga you been feenin' for."

I said as I danced in the seat while we waited for the valet service the club had.

"Okay miss thang. Somebody decided to let loose I see and you're right I'm ready to spend some time with him tonight. But you gotta make sure I don't do no dumb shit"

"You know I got your back girl." I reassured her.

The valet came out and Shanice handed him the keys. We walked up to the doorman and Shanice gave him her name and said she had a plus one also. He didn't check our ID's or anything. He just waved us through and told us to have a nice night. There wasn't a line since this was by invite only.

As we walked in we made our way down a level of steps to enter the club. The inside of the place was all dark brown and black colors, from the wood floor and steps to the elegant black marble bars that were placed around the walls. The dance floor was down another level of steps and there was a balcony above us looking over everything.

I had to admit the atmosphere of the club was relaxed and mature. There was good music playing and plenty of people dancing to keep it from being boring either. We made our way over to the bar and stood back to take in our surroundings some more.

I assumed the upper level was the VIP section since there was tables and bottle service up there. Everything was really clean and upscale in here. The place was packed but not uncomfortable where you had to rub shoulders with everybody. Most of the men were dressed in suits and the women were in dressy club attire.

I asked Shanice where she was supposed to meet the man who had convinced her to come and she just shrugged her shoulders. We decided to enjoy ourselves in the meantime and ordered a shot of Hennessy each. We downed the shots and then Shanice grabbed my hand to pull me down on the dance floor.

As we made our way to the dance floor niggas were trying to hollar, but we just kept walking like we owned the place. I couldn't stand thirsty niggas anyway it was like they were desperate and the last thing I wanted was a needy man. We knew we were the best looking women in the building tonight. I hadn't seen another bitch in here that was anywhere close to looking as good as we did. We were getting the stares from them too but the look they gave us was one of envy and hate something we were used to. Fuck them. We were about to really make them mad.

We danced for a few songs until we needed a break and wanted another drink. Me and Shanice went back over to the bar. Before we could order another drink the man who had given me his card earlier made his way over to where we were standing. I was feeling the effects of the alcohol and weed and instantly smiled when he came near. He wrapped his arm around my waist putting his body in full contact with mine and spoke low into my ear.

"I see we meet again beautiful it must be fate."

His lips being so close to my ear gave me goosebumps. I was horny as hell ever since being around Messiah's ass last night and the alcohol didn't help. Shamar was sexy but he didn't have anywhere near the same effect on me that Messiah did. Here I was thinking about him again even while another nigga was in my face.

All of the sudden, I saw a fist come out of nowhere and connect with the side of Shamar's head knocking him down instantly. The shit almost took me down in the process since his arm was around my waist. The impact caused me to stumble before I regained my balance. I instantly turned around looking for Shanice ready to get the fuck up out of here and that's when I locked eyes with none other than Messiah's ass.

He looked like a crazed man. His eyes were dark and he smiled at me like he hadn't just knocked someone the fuck out right next to me. He looked down at Shamar and bent down low to where he was able to grab a hold of his face as he was laid out on the floor. He slapped him a few times and then started talking shit to him.

"Wake up, wake up mothafucka." He demanded.

Shamar made a grumbling noise and his eyes fluttered back open. He still seemed out of it but Messiah wasn't through with him yet apparently.

"You see this woman? The woman you felt the need to put your fuckin' hands on and talk to? You bet not ever in your fuckin' life touch what belongs to me again nigga. You know who I am and how I get down. Take this as your one and only warning."

Messiah let the Shamar's head drop back down on the floor and stepped over him like it was nothing. I was looking on and by this time my buzz was completely gone. I was stuck in place and couldn't seem to move. I knew I should be intimidated by what I just saw but my mind and body wasn't cooperating.

All I could think about was how fine this man was looking instead of worrying about Shamar or being scared like I should have been. He was dressed in a black suit and looked good from head to toe. I wanted to feel his hands on me again and have him kiss me like he did last night.

I felt bad for Shamar because he really hadn't done anything to deserve what Messiah did to him and I would make sure to apologize to him if I ever ran into him again. While I was stuck thinking about Messiah, he took a few steps closer to me and said in a hard voice,

"Let's go LaLa, you know I warned you 'bout this shit earlier, but you out showing your ass I see. What the

fuck you got on? Letting all these niggas see my shit."
he let out as he tugged at the bottom of my dress.

He wrapped his arm around my waist and walked me
over to who I assumed were his friends. It wasn't normal
how he switched up from being a damn maniac one
minute who laid a man out for just touching me and then
was all calm like nothing even happened.

When we approached the group I noticed Shanice
was standing among them. She was smiling in one of the
men's faces like she knew him and he was whispering in
her ear. I figured this must have been the mystery man
she had been talking about since she would never be up
close and personal with some random ass nigga. She
was way too picky for that and would dismiss anyone
who even attempted to approach her.

Messiah introduced me to his friend Draco first and
then Silk who was the one Shanice was talking to. I
found out that everyone really called Messiah Money
because they kept calling him it, and his ass answered
them.

Then Messiah led the way up to the VIP section on
the top level where they had a section reserved. Up in
VIP me and Shanice had another drink and danced while
we stood near the balcony overlooking the dance floor
below.

I was swaying my hips back and forth to the beat of
the song playing when I felt Messiah come up behind
me. He leaned in close and began kissing on my neck
while he pressed himself closer to me. I felt his hard
dick on my ass as I continued to dance on him.

After that shit Messiah was ready to leave and I
ended up leaving right along with him. He somehow
convinced me it was a good idea. I made sure Shanice
was okay and she was sober enough to know what she

was doing. Silk was going to make sure that she got home safe and we planned on texting each other to be sure.

Messiah wanted me to go back to his place with him. For some reason I felt comfortable enough with him to agree. He promised not to try anything I wasn't ready for and I believed him. I didn't trust him but I did feel he was honest at least. I was willing to see where things went between us because I couldn't deny the attraction I had for him even if I wanted to.

His home was located just out of the city limits in a nice ass neighborhood. I realized he must really have some money and be pretty big in the streets if he had two cars and a home at nineteen years old. He told me he had just bought this new Audi this morning to celebrate a business deal he made.

I wasn't dumb and even though I was inexperienced. I knew he was selling drugs. I figured it wasn't something that would impact what we had going on. It wasn't a big enough problem for me to not talk to him and get to know him better at least.

The house was a nice two story home that had a white exterior. When he led me inside I could see that he kept a clean house but it definitely lacked a female's touch. That made me feel relieved on the inside. All of his furniture was either black or white and I thought that fit him well from what I had seen so far.

"Come here LaLa. Stop acting all shy and shit." Messiah called to me from the living room.

I was still standing in the entry way stuck in my thoughts. I slowly walked over to the couch and sat down next to him. He bent down to the floor and grabbed my feet. I looked at him like he was crazy.

"Why you grabbing my feet?" I asked as he began to take my heels off.

He then lifted them up and slowly guided my legs and whole body so that I was in a leaned back position. Then he placed my feet in his lap and began massaging them.

"I know these pretty ass feet hurt with them high ass heels you had on. You looked fucking perfect tonight in the little ass dress you got on. You lucky I didn't take you in the bathroom and fuck the shit out of you." Messiah said.

I just sat back and enjoyed the feeling of his hands rubbing on my feet. The way he talked nasty to me was turning me on so I was trying to ignore what he was saying. I continued to watch his hands work as my mind and body became more relaxed and horny.

"So you ready to let a nigga claim you LaLa?"

"I'm scared of being hurt Messiah. We just met yesterday. I mean I feel like we got a good connection. But we don't even know each other yet." I said honestly.

I wanted to tell him exactly how I was feeling so he would know where I stood. All this shit was moving so fast. We just met and now here I was at his house with him massaging my feet like we had known each other forever.

"Stop thinking so much. Does it feel right LaLa? You know a nigga got you. I'm not going nowhere ma. I'm all yours, you just gotta let me in." Messiah said with a look that told me he was being honest too.

"Okay, but you better not fuck me over Messiah."

I looked him deep in the eyes to let him know that I was willing to open up but I wasn't about to put up with no bullshit. As long as he kept shit real with me and had my back that was good enough for me. It felt so right to be here with him now in this moment. So I was just going to go with it for now.

I leaned back further on the couch and closed my eyes so I could fully relax. Messiah stopped massaging my feet began massaging my calves making his way up to my thighs with his hands. It felt so amazing and I wanted him to keep going so I opened my legs wider to give him a better view of my thong.

He brought his hands further up while kissing on my legs, then lifted my dress. He pulled my thong down and took the shit right off and I didn't protest. His hands found their way to my pussy and he spread my lips while he rubbing on my clit with his thumb.

I was in heaven and my body was loving the attention. His face was so close to my pussy that I could feel his breath, turning me on even more.

"Damn this the prettiest pussy I ever seen". This my pussy LaLa, you hear me?

"Mmhmm it's yours." I managed to get out.

Then he dove right in with his tongue finding my clit. I started feeling like he was sucking the soul out of me and my body could hardly take it. I let the feelings take over and began to ride his face while I laid back enjoying this sexy ass nigga using his mouth to please me.

I never got an orgasm from a nigga eating my pussy, but he had me ready to cum at any moment. He lifted his head and stopped all of the sudden. I opened my eyes to see why the hell he stopped when I was so close.

"Look at me while I eat this pretty ass pussy LaLa. This my pussy right?

I couldn't say a word so I just shook my head yes.

"I want you to see what the fuck I'm doing to you. Your pussy tastes so fucking good."

I watched him put his mouth back on my clit and begin sucking on it hard as hell. The whole time never taking his eyes off mine. Then he started using his fingers to open me up which had me going wild from the sensations. My body responded instantly and before I knew it I was cumming. Messiah just kept on sucking until he had licked every drop of my cum.

When he finally finished he sat up to take off his shirt. I saw he had a tattoo on his stomach of some quote but I couldn't make it out since the lights were low. Then he stepped out of his shoes and set them to the side. He followed up by taking off his pants and then his boxers.

Messiah's body was perfect to me. He had broad shoulders, strong arms and a chiseled stomach. His dick was standing at attention and had my mouth watering, but the shit was huge. I didn't know what to do with it. He stepped back over to the couch and pulled the dress all the way over my head while his dick was near my face. When I say his shit was huge, it was thick and long as hell.

His cocky ass just said, "You gonna take this big ass dick ma." Now come suck your dick. This your dick right?" He challenged.

I only sucked dick one time before and it was probably half the size of Messiah's but I watched plenty of pornos to have an idea of what I wanted to do. I dropped to my knees and took the tip of his dick in my mouth. I let the spit build up and drip down making it extra sloppy. I licked the bottom of his long dick from the tip to his balls before I began a steady rhythm of sucking. I kept flicking my tongue around the tip each time as I continued to move my mouth up and down his dick.

I massaged his balls with one of my hands while he gripped my hair. He must have liked the head I was giving because he started fucking my face harder. His dick was so big that I was just about choking with tears in my eyes, but the shit was still turning me on. So with my other hand I began to play in my pussy while I looked up at Messiah. He was staring down at me with an intense look. With him watching me I went harder and used my jaws to suck and slurp faster.

"Just like that, fuck you 'bout to make me cum." I heard him say.

He pulled his dick out of my mouth and told me to lay down. I laid down like he told me to do. Messiah got down between my legs and forced his dick into my pussy in one motion. I yelled out because the shit hurt so bad even though I knew it was coming. Damn it was too big and I felt like he tore me in half.

"Shhh, don't move LaLa, it'll feel better in a minute. Relax, let your pussy get used to this big dick."

Messiah moved in slow circular motions. He took my breasts in both of his hands and began kissing and sucking on them which soon had me forgetting all about the pain. He started to slide his dick in and out of me faster until I was moaning from how good it was feeling. The shit still hurt every time he was all the way in, but the pain had me wanting more. It felt good as hell and the more I let my body relax and get into the feelings the harder Messiah was fucking me. You could hear the wetness that was dripping from me every time he was all the way in.

"Messiah I can't take no more, Oh my God what are you doing to me?"

I was scratching his back and screaming. I started moving my hips more and more to match him.

"That's right fuck me back. Damn La your pussy so tight. I wanna see you cum on my dick."

His words had me turned on more, making me cum again. Messiah backed up and flipped me over so that I was on all fours. He cupped each of my ass cheeks and spread them apart. Then he began to eat my pussy from the back, using his tongue to replace his dick. One of his hands gripped my ass and the other found my clit. I felt myself cumming again and as soon as I was finished he stuck his dick back in.

"Fuck! Shit!" was all I could get out as he continued to fuck me slow and deep making sure I felt every inch of his dick. I really didn't think I could handle any more of what he was doing to me.

"Don't run from the dick, take it. This your dick, fuck me back. Let me see that ass bounce."

He was in my fucking stomach but all I wanted was more of everything he was making me feel. So I started bouncing my ass just like I did when I danced except now I was doing it on his big ass dick. I made sure to take all of him in each time he dug in deep.

Messiah grabbed ahold of my hips and pulled me back so that his dick was planted as deep in me as it could go. I screamed out before my whole body tensed up and I cummed again. Messiah took a few more strokes before he finished and released inside of me. Then he slowly slid out and I instantly missed his dick. It was like my body was already craving more of what it had just been given by this man.

I had just given up my virginity to a man I met yesterday. I hoped he didn't think I was a hoe. But no matter what he thought of me now, I didn't regret what had happened one bit. I was already in love with the feeling of him inside me so there wasn't a chance I would be stopping anytime soon unless he fucked up. I wasn't a fool and I knew we weren't in a real relationship so maybe we could just stay friends with benefits.

Messiah (Money)

What the fuck had I gotten myself into with this girl? We were laying in my big ass king size bed. I was awake and Larissa was sound asleep next to me. This was the house I kept out of town. The one I never took bitches to period. But here I was not only entertaining a female in my home but laying up with one too. This shit was all the way out of my character and now I was trying to figure out how I was gonna handle shit from here on out.

I had no idea LaLa was a fucking virgin. I mean she was fine as hell and her body was on a whole other fucking level. I couldn't see why another nigga had let her get away without fucking first at least. I didn't even plan on trying no shit tonight and only wanted her company when I asked her to come home with me. But once she said she was gonna let a nigga in I had to claim what was mine.

Her pussy was perfect too and when I saw that shit it was a done fucking deal. Shit she even tasted like fresh mango and her pussy was nice and fat the way I liked. I could tell she took care of herself which turned me on more. As soon as I put my dick in I knew I had fucked up. Her pussy was so fucking tight but it was too late to stop even if I wanted to.

There wasn't no way I would take that shit back though. The fact that she hadn't been with another nigga made that shit even better. I was feeling like I would want to body any nigga who had even touched her before me. I was ready to wake her ass up right now and go another round or two but figured she was probably too sore. I was a young nigga with a big sexual appetite

77

and was used to feeling pussy at least twice a day if not more.

I couldn't believe she took all eleven inches and had me feeling like a bitch about to cum early. Once she got used to my size she started fucking me back like a champ. Her pussy was out of this fucking world. Maybe it was because I knew it wasn't tainted with no other nigga's dick or because she was tight and gushing wet the whole time we was fucking. Either way, there was no way I was letting her ass go. She was mine whether she liked that shit or not.

I had to make sure she understood what it meant to be with a boss ass nigga like me. I knew for a fact she was green to all this street shit. She was a good girl and I was far from one of those square ass niggas she was used to dealing with.

Even though I just met shorty I felt like we could build something. She was the type of woman I needed in my life to balance me out. I just had to find a way to make shit work with her and keep my operation moving ahead. I wasn't gonna let anything or anyone get in the way of making money.

I looked down at my phone and saw a bunch of missed calls from Carina and a few texts from Chyna. It was already four thirty in the morning and in a few hours I would be catching my flight out to Charlotte. I shut my phone off and rolled over wrapping my arms around Larissa. I wasn't in no rush to hear Carina's bitching and wasn't looking to fuck so there was no point in talking to either of them right now.

I never slept with a bitch through the night. I always fucked and left so I didn't give the wrong impression. I never wifed these hoes so I don't know why Carina would think she was different. This shit right here with

LaLa felt right though and I wanted her ass right here with me in my bed. She was definitely about to become wifey.

It seemed like as soon as my head hit the pillow I was waking up to my alarm going off. I reached over and turned it off and realized Larissa wasn't in bed next to me anymore. I stood up and heard the shower running so I knew she was at least still here and hadn't tried to run off on my ass.

After using the bathroom down the hall I came back in and made my way into the bathroom. I opened the shower door and stepped in behind LaLa's sexy ass. I began rubbing on her back taking my time to massage her shoulders, working my way slowly down until I was rubbing her ass that was sitting up right. My dick was already hard.

So I lifted her leg and placed it on the ledge. I put her hands up against the front wall of the shower. Larissa looked back over her shoulder at me with a sexy ass smirk letting me know she was ready for the dick. I slid the mothafucka in from the back and took my time working my way in since her pussy clamping down on my shit. I was on a mission to make her ass remember the way my dick felt while I was gone. When I was finished with LaLa her pussy was gonna be fit to my dick, even the curve.

Once my dick was completely in I wrapped my arm around LaLa and pulled her back to me even more. I knew my dick was in them damn guts from the way she screamed out my name. I was gonna show her who she was really fucking with before I told her. Last night I went easy on her since it was her first time. But now she needed to take the dick.

I sped up and began pounding her pussy. I was digging her out, showing no mercy while she was throwing that fat ass back making it bounce with each stroke. Since I had a whole ledge in my stand up shower. I picked her ass up while I sat down.

I slid Larissa down on my dick while her legs wrapped around my waist. I held her down so she couldn't go nowhere. She had her hands on my shoulders gripping the hell out them. I knew my dick was a big mothafucka but she was gonna learn to take all of it. I had LaLa where she couldn't do nothing but take this monster.

I gripped her ass cheeks hard as hell and started lifting her up and down so she was riding my dick the way I wanted her to. I used the grip I had on her ass to let my dick dig deeper each time she came all the way down. Her screams got louder and she kept saying she couldn't take no more but all that did was make me go even harder.

Larissa's juices were coating my dick making it extra slippery with the shower water running over us.

"You like that shit LaLa? Take all this mothafucka. Show me how much my pussy loves this dick. Ride it ma"

"Yes Messiah, Yes. It's so fucking big! Damn I'm about to cum!"

LaLa leaned her head back and started bouncing up and down just like I told her. Her pussy was gripping my shit more and more with her big ass titties right in my face. I squeezed them and began sucking on each one while she was putting in work. Then I began sucking on her neck while still playing with her nipples. I was trying to leave a damn mark so every nigga would know she was mine and off limits.

She had me ready to bust so I grabbed a hold of her hips and held her in place for a minute while my dick was sunk deep inside her. The shit was turning us both on more and I could feel her pussy muscles tightening around me. We stared into each other's eyes until we were both cumming.

I never let a woman take my nut like that while I was sober. It was like we were mentally on some different type of shit. I knew it was too soon and I probably shouldn't be fucking her without pulling out. The crazy part was that I was like fuck it. If her ass got pregnant with my seed I would be cool with it even though we had just started fucking around. There was no way I was about to wear a condom with her ass, and pulling out wasn't an option since I wanted her to take the nut. It was just something about her that had me wanting to give her everything.

I lifted her from my lap and we took our time washing each other before getting out of the shower. She didn't have any other clothes to change into since she came with me from the club last night. So I gave her a pair of my shorts and a black wife beater. LaLa didn't wear a bra last night so I could see her hard nipples through my shirt and the baller shorts were sexy as fuck on her too since she had all that ass filling them up. My dick was hard all over again but I knew that there wasn't any time for us to fuck again since I promised her breakfast before I dropped her off.

We headed out and made our way across town to a small diner that had some good ass breakfast food.

"They got the best pancakes here. I know your ass gonna love them." I said as we were being seated in a booth.

"Yeah, okay. I'll try them but they better be good or it's your ass." Larissa said with that same cocky ass smirk she had earlier.

Even without makeup she was a ten. I sat across from LaLa and admired her natural beauty for a minute before the waitress came over and took our orders. Once we ordered, I decided now was the time where I would lay some real shit out there and see how LaLa would react. There was certain things she needed to know about me if we were going to move forward with any type of relationship.

"LaLa I got some shit I need to explain."

Before I got another word out the waitress came back and put our drinks down on the table. We both ordered a coffee and water. I drank mine black but LaLa was in the process of putting a lot of damn sugar and cream in hers. She had a worried look on her face like she was preparing herself to hear some bad shit from me. While she fixed her coffee, I started back telling her what was up.

"I'm a boss ass nigga in these streets. I'm gonna keep shit real with you cus I want you to be my woman. I have a certain type of lifestyle and I need you to understand that to be with a man like me ain't gonna be easy. You gotta be on your grown woman shit and hold a nigga down no matter what. There's gonna be times when I'm out of town or can't be reached because I'm handling shit that needs to be dealt with no questions asked. At the end of the day, I'm all about my money. Now the shit I do I'll keep away from you, but you gotta decide if you can handle being with a thug like me."

She took her time sipping on her coffee while listening to every word I said. I could tell she was thinking shit over before she responded and I appreciated that shit. The fact that she was smart enough to take time out and listen before she gave an answer proved she wasn't just another birdbrain bitch. Too many bitches liked to run their mouths without thinking about the dumb shit that they said.

"I'm willing to see where this goes. But you gotta be honest with me. If we're just gonna be friends and fuck then let me know. If we gonna be on some exclusive relationship shit let me know. I don't fuck around and I'm not trying to put my heart into something just to get fucked over. If I'm down for you, I would never turn my back on you. Trust and loyalty is very important to me so I expect the same in return. The street shit I know nothing about. But whatever you need me to be I can do that as long as you have my back." LaLa finished as our food arrived.

Damn shorty had bossed up on my ass. Everything she said let me know she was the real fucking deal. She wasn't some groupie hoe that was after my money and she wouldn't let me walk all over her. I didn't want a weak ass woman. I wanted a lady who would be by my side and hold me down without question and she was all that and more.

"I got you shorty. We about to do this shit. Your mine now and we gonna definitely be on some exclusive shit. I'm not letting another nigga even look at you." I told her ass and I was serious as hell.

We started eating and just like I told her the pancakes were good as fuck. Over breakfast we started talking more about our families. She told me she missed her sister and brother and how her parents were both on some other shit and didn't give a fuck about her basically. I realized why she had a hard time with trust since her own parents had fucked her over. I let her know about my mama and brothers. How we were tight as hell and my big bro had gotten picked up and was down serving time in the feds.

We sat and chopped it up for about an hour before leaving. I told her I was gonna be out of town for a few days and we could facetime and shit. She seemed fine with me leaving and said she had lot of school work to do anyway. After dropping Larissa off at her mother's house again I made my way over to the airport to catch my flight.

When I arrived at the airport Draco and Silk were already standing by the gate ready to go through security. I checked in and made my way over to my niggas. We each had separate flights but our departure times were within a half hour of each other. We planned to meet up to make sure shit was still a go.

After we passed through security we sat down and waited to catch our flights. We would be out of contact with each other for a few days, except to discuss necessary shit. It was important to limit what we spoke about over the phone even if we used coded messages.

Shanice

"Bitch, I got some shit to tell you about last night. Can you believe this mothafucka had some dusty ass hoe step to me after ya'll left?" I was damn near yelling into the phone as I talked to Larissa.

"Girl what in the world happened? When I left with Messiah you two seemed happy. All touchy feely and smiling in each other's faces and shit."

"Some stripper looking bitch came up to us and pushed me away from Silk. Then started talking shit to him saying how he wasn't shit to be out with a bitch while she was waiting for him at home."

I was beyond mad at Silk but mostly with myself for being stupid enough to even have agreed to meet up with that disrespectful ass nigga. Especially since I had heard about how he was a damn hoe out here. My dumb ass still gave him the benefit of the doubt. It was definitely a mistake that I wouldn't be making again.

"Neesy what did you do when that bitch showed her ass?" Larissa asked.

"I didn't do shit to that nasty bitch or that hoe ass nigga. He's not my nigga to be fighting over in the first place. She can have his dog ass. Before they even finished their argument I walked away and took my ass home. Wasn't no way I was about to stand there looking dumb as hell for some shit that nigga chose to do."

"I'm sorry friend. I know you was feeling him for real. Don't worry though it's his loss and the next nigga's gain," she said.

I was already over the shit though and wasn't worrying about Silk's dumb ass anymore. He fucked up and I didn't do second chances.

"Thanks bestie. Enough about that stupid nigga. What happened with you and Money when ya'll left?"

"We went back to his house and he fucked the shit out of me that's what happened. And I guess I'm his woman now or so he says."

I could hear the excitement mixed with worry in her voice. My best bitch finally got some dick and was in a damn relationship that quick. I was so happy for her. It was time she let her guard down and hopefully she could find love.

"I want details bitch."

"Well he took me back to his place and one thing led to another. I was scared to death once I saw how big his dick was but there was no stopping once he was eating my pussy. Then I almost died when we started, but by the end the shit felt amazing. Girl we even fucked again this morning in the shower. If I would have known sex felt so good I would have been fucking. Damn I'm gonna miss the way the dick feel while he's gone." Larissa ended.

"Finally my bitch got dicked down properly. We have to celebrate!"

"Uh uh, I'm tired as hell. Girl I'm about to curl up in my bed and sleep the rest of the day."

"Good dick will do that to you." I said as we both laughed.

Once we hung up the phone, I sat around thinking some more about what a fucked up situation I had been put in last night. I got my hopes up just to be let down. I knew better, but Silk had talked me into giving him a chance. I just knew I was gonna see that dumb mothafucka again since I spent time in the hood and now that my girl was with his friend we were bound to cross paths. I swear he better not even fucking look my way again. Whatever we might have had was out the window now. I wouldn't be a fool twice that was for damn sure.

Larissa

It had been almost a week since Money left out of town. We only talked twice and face timed once. I missed him so much but wouldn't let him know that. It was crazy how he was always on my mind since we hadn't even gotten to spend much time together. I was also feeling a little insecure. I mean we had fucked, then made it official, and right after it was like he up and left.

Messiah told me he was in the streets and a boss nigga. He let me know up front what it would be like. So I shouldn't be feeling some type of way I guess. But it seemed to me like he wasn't concerned with me at all while he was gone and he was all I thought about. My body was missing him too. I would replay the few times we had sex over and over again in my head while playing in my pussy to get some relief. I was so glad he got back last night and was more than ready to see him.

The hickey on my neck was almost completely faded so I opted not to cover it up with foundation today. It was Saturday and I was stuck in the house since Shanice wasn't feeling well. I usually tried to stay in my room while my mother was away at the hospital. But my stomach was rumbling with hunger. I decided to go into the kitchen and make a peanut butter and jelly sandwich real quick.

While I was standing at the counter fixing my plate I felt someone's presence behind me. I turned around and was startled to see my stepfather was only about a foot away from me. He had an evil ass look on his face while he smiled at me. I backed up as far as I could into the counter to put some more space between us.

"Look at the nigger bitch thinking she's too good to come out here and spend some time with her daddy."

I ignored his comment and turned back around to finish making my sandwich. He was scaring the shit out of me and I was shaking trying to hurry the hell up so I could get out of the kitchen and back to my room. My step father Jim was a big guy. He stood over six feet tall and had a big ass beer belly. He was disgusting in every way. He even smelled bad.

Before I knew what was happening, Jim pulled at my pajama shorts making them come down. Then he grabbed my hips pulling me back into his fat ass. I felt his little dick touching my ass while he was trying to get it near my pussy. There was no way this mothafucka was about to stick his nasty ass dick in me and rape me without me putting up a fight.

I didn't stop to think as I took the butter knife I was using to make my sandwich and spun around trying to stab him with it in the neck. I cut through the flesh of his neck but not very deep since it was butter knife. He stumbled back and grabbed at his neck which was now bleeding with his pants still around his ankles. I quickly pulled my shorts back up and ran into my room, grabbed my phone and purse and left out of the house immediately. There was no way I would be returning with that perverted ass man still there.

I began walking down the sidewalk still in my pajamas, not even with shoes on my feet. I couldn't believe some shit like this had really happened and my mother's husband tried to rape me. I called Shanice back to back but she didn't answer. I figured she was asleep since she was sick. The only other person I knew to call who was around was Messiah. He had gotten back in town late last night and called me when he made it home. I dialed his number frantically with my adrenalin still pumping.

"Hey, Messiah can you pick me up?" I let out.

"Where the fuck you at, what happened?" He yelled into the phone making it sound like he was mad at me or something.

"I'm walking down the sidewalk by my house towards the gas station on the corner." I quietly replied.

"Stay where you at LaLa. I'll be there in a minute."

I guess all I could do was stand here and wait for Messiah to pick me up. I had no one else to call who could help me out. I didn't want Money to see me like this but I couldn't stay out here either.

Messiah (Money)

I was over at Carina's house. We just finished fucking when Larissa called my phone. I knew I wasn't shit for telling Larissa we were exclusive, while I was still out fucking other bitches. But there was no way I was gonna let her be out here single and have another nigga come in the picture. I wanted her ass to myself. I would eventually tell her about Carina being pregnant but all the fucking I was doing on the side I would make sure she didn't find out about. Shit I was young and I wanted it all.

As soon as I picked up the phone Carina decided to be on her petty shit. She dropped down to her knees and began sucking my dick. She knew what the fuck she was doing too damn and it felt good as fuck. When I heard how upset LaLa sounded I knew something was wrong. I was going to go scoop her up and find out exactly what the fuck happened that had her crying.

Once I hung up I let Carina continue sucking my dick since she started that shit. She was going all the way out today trying to prove a point. So I grabbed the back of her head and moved her mouth faster making sure she was taking all my dick down her throat. I didn't care if the bitch choked or not since she wanted to play games with me while I was on the phone. Of course she kept going without hesitation.

"Suck that shit harder. Keep it sloppy ma."

Carina did exactly what I fucking told her and put her mouth to work even more. I felt my nut building and pulled out as my cum shot out and landed all over her face.

I didn't bother to wipe my dick off as I put my clothes back on because I was ready to go see about LaLa. Carina wanted me to come over so we could talk about the baby and she ended up pulling my dick out and sitting on it within the first five minutes I was here. So now there was no need for a discussion. It was obvious she just wanted some of this monster dick and I was happy to break her off. But now, I needed to go pick my woman up and make sure she was straight.

"So you just gonna leave out for another bitch Money like I don't mean shit to you? What about the baby?" Carina had the nerve to ask.

"You wasn't worried about the baby when you was hopping on my dick as soon as I walked in the door. Why you worried now? And don't ever let me hear you call my woman a bitch. Now get the fuck out of my face Carina. You served your purpose ma."

"Really you're gonna just walk out like we don't have nothing! I'm not some random bitch you can fuck anytime you feel like it. I'm having your baby nigga. I'm your woman, not some next bitch who you barely know."

As soon as Carina let the word bitch come out of her mouth again I yoked her ass up against the wall.

"You lucky you're pregnant Carina. You know I don't do that disrespect shit. If I say something I mean it. I kill mothafuckas for less." I had to let her know her place. This bitch must have forgot who the fuck I was.

"I'm sorry Money. You know I love you and I'm not about to let another girl have what's mine." Carina was crying but I didn't have time for this shit.

I finished gathering my belongings and ignored Carina's fake as crocodile tears as I left out. She would have to get in line or there was going to be consequences. Wasn't nobody getting in the way of the shit I had planned in the streets or what I had planned for me and LaLa.

When I turned into Larissa's neighborhood I spotted her right away. She was standing on the sidewalk in front of a house down the road from where she stayed. She didn't even have shoes on her feet and she had some small ass pajama shorts on with a tank top that I could see her nipples through. Damn my dick was getting hard looking at her already. I wasn't going to disrespect her by fucking with her without washing first though.

I pulled up in front of where she was standing and instantly could tell something was off. It was obvious she had been crying and her body was shaking as she lowered herself into the seat beside me. I tried to touch her arm and get her to look at me but she pulled away staring straight ahead.

"What the fuck happened Larissa?" I asked.

"My stepdad, he…" she got out before she broke down crying again.

"He what?" my angered flared.

I already knew he had tried something but I needed to know exactly what. I would be sure to make him pay for the shit he tried.

"He came up behind me in the kitchen, called me a nigger, then before I could stop him, he pulled my shorts down and tried to rape me. Oh my God, I have nowhere to go! What am I gonna do?"

She was crying harder now, and had her hands covering her eyes with her head down. The shit she told me had me ready to body that mothafucka. I put in a call to my boys to help me make shit happen. After ending the call with Silk I turned Larissa's head to look at me.

"I got you ma. I'm gonna take care of you LaLa. You're with a boss. I got you."

LaLa nodded her head like she was accepting the shit I was saying and reclined her seat to lay back. She closed her eyes and let her arm rest over her face. Not long after I saw my niggas pull up and park right in front of LaLa's house up the street like I had instructed them to do. I hopped out of my car and jogged over to where they were parked. I told them to pop the trunk and wait for me to come back out in a minute.

I walked up to the front door and knocked twice. Once that fat mothafucka opened the door I kicked it all the way in causing him to step back a few feet. I made my way in and closed the door. I pulled out my gun from the back of my pants and pressed that shit against his temple. The fat mothafucka dropped to his knees and started crying like the bitch he was. I kept my anger in check while I was in the car with LaLa so she wouldn't see that side of me. But now I had this sick mothafucka who touched what was my woman right in front of me.

"Don't cry now mothafucka, you wanted to touch what's mine. Trying to rape your own step daughter. What the fuck's wrong with you?"

I took my Ruger and slapped him across the face with the butt of the gun. Blood started seeping from his mouth. Somehow he decided to get some courage and looked up at me with an evil ass grin on his face.

"I almost got that little bitch too. I bet she would have loved having some white meat. She would've been begging for it once I started." He began to laugh. "Next time I'll get that black pussy and make her call me daddy."

The thought of this man even laying a finger on LaLa in the first place was pissing me the fuck off. Now she was out in my ride crying because of some sick shit he tried to pull. Then he decided to get bold all the sudden and wanted to talk shit too. Nah this racist ass mothafucka was about to die. I wasn't about to let this shit slide.

"There won't be a next time."

I punched him in the face and dropped him, knocking him out cold. I lifted him up and dragged his ass out the front door with him upright. I wasn't worried about anyone seeing me. He wasn't putting up a fight and it just looked like some Cousin Vinny shit. I placed him in the trunk and closed it before telling Draco and Silk to take him to the warehouse.

Walking back over to where my car was parked I noticed Larissa had gotten herself together some which had me feeling relieved. I wasn't an emotional nigga and didn't know how to comfort her. I cared about LaLa more than I had ever cared about a woman, other than my mother. When she told me what happened I knew the feelings I had for her went deeper than I thought. She had me ready to body any mothafucka that laid a finger on her. When I began to drive off Larissa looked over at me.

"Thank you Messiah for having my back. I don't want you to think I'm weak and can't handle shit on my own. But thanks for being here."

Every time she spoke she drew me in more. Here she had just gone through some real shit and she was thanking me. I could tell she was used to doing shit on her own and not having someone to look out for her which made me want to protect her more.

"LaLa I'm here for good, I'm not going nowhere. We in this shit. You can't get rid of me if you wanted to. I'm about to drop you at my house for a while. I'll be back later with clothes and shit you'll need. Your ass staying with me and I don't want to hear shit about it."

LaLa sat back in her seat and we rode in silence all the way back to my house. When we were inside I had Larissa go up to my bedroom and lay down. I knew she was still upset and trying to get past what happened earlier so I tucked her in under the covers and went to leave out. She began to kiss me slow while I was leaned over her. She had my dick hard and I knew her ass wanted some dick too. But I couldn't fuck with her right now.

Not after I had been at Carina's and hadn't washed her pussy off my dick yet. So I pulled away before shit got too far and told her I would be back in a little while. I hurried my ass on and made my way out to the warehouse.

Draco and Silk were ready and waiting for me when I pulled up. I wanted to handle this mothafucka and make him suffer for the shit he put my girl through. He wasn't about to get a quick easy death. Larissa's step father was chained up hanging ass naked with his mouth gagged as I approached.

My niggas knew I liked this killing shit. But I made sure to only body someone when it was necessary. I didn't want to get caught up for something dumb. The shit he did to Larissa was worth taking the risk. Plus our facility was equipped with chloroform so we could let a body disintegrate without a trace of DNA anywhere. We didn't need a cleanup crew when we could handle shit on our own. When we expanded we would need to make sure other niggas on our team could handle their own shit too without tying it to us in any way.

I took my time walking slowly over to the table where I kept all kinds of tools to torture a person with. I picked up my favorite, my machete. I went right up to his ass and used the machete to cut off his dick in one slice. He passed out from the pain instantly. I wanted him to wake up and realize what the fuck had happened and who the fuck I was before I killed him though. I wanted to make sure he experienced enough pain for touching Larissa.

So I used the taser to get his ass to wake the hell up. Once his eyes popped back open, I cut off each of his arms then his legs with the machete. He screamed and eventually went unconscious from the pain and loss of blood again. His body was in pieces on the floor while his torso was still hanging. I took my nine and let off a few in his dome just to make sure the sick fucker was dead.

Draco and Silk were sitting back laughing when I finished. They were standing by smoking the whole time they watched me put in work. They knew not to fuck with me when I was zoned out and about to torture a mothafucka.

"Damn bruh, you had to chop that fat asses dick off and all. What the fuck he do?" Draco asked while shaking his head.

"He tried to fuck with my girl. You know he sealed his fate with that shit." I answered.

"Alright let's get rid of the body" Silk said as he made his way over to the chains to let the body down, or what was left of it.

Then he went over to a barrel of chloroform we kept in the corner. One by one we placed the body parts in the barrel. It was a slow process but worth the time. When we were finished cleaning up I went to take a shower in my office. Now that my girl was staying with me, I had to be careful about how I moved with the bitches I was fucking around with. I knew if she found out it would be over for us. I could see that I was going to have to become a one woman nigga to keep her but I just wasn't ready yet. She was definitely worth trying for eventually. I washed my dick extra so there wasn't a trace of Carina's pussy scent left anywhere.

Me and the boys had our first shipment coming in tomorrow from the new deal. Each of us were successful in setting up a trap house in the cities without a problem. The niggas we chose to work for us were recommended by our current team members or family. We only had three niggas working each trap to keep the shit small and under the radar. I knew with the setup we had it would be no problem getting rid of the product before the two month deadline.

Now all we needed to do was stay on top of shit here in Wilmington and keep in contact with our workers out in the other cities. One of us three would fly out weekly switching up each time and hit every city to make sure shit was being done the right way. Everything was coming together and we would be making millions in a couple months. After that we would continue until we ran the state. I had plans to pull together the business side of the operation in the meantime. It was time for us to build this shit up into more than an operation but a fucking empire.

It was around six when I left the warehouse and started home. I stopped by the mall on the way and dropped a few bands buying LaLa all the shit I thought she would need. I even went into Victoria's Secret to get her shit I knew she would like. Bitches in the stores were flocking to me. I couldn't do nothing but shake my head.

I was asking this sexy ass sales associate if they had another size in some pants I picked out for my girl. The next thing I knew she had me in the dressing room with my pants around my ankles. She was on her knees sucking the shit out of my dick. I didn't know this bitch's name or anything but I would bless her with this big monster if she wanted it. She could catch my nut but that was all she could get.

She used her lips to suction my dick as her head moved back and forth. She wasn't trying to deep throat my shit but shit she wanted to take the dick without even asking so I was going to make her take it. I grabbed the back of the bitch's head forcefully with both of my hands and began to pump in and out, shoving it all in. She was gagging and choking but she kept sucking. I didn't feel the need to say shit to the bitch. She wanted to act like a hoe so I was going to treat her like one. I wanted to hurry up and get this nut out so I pictured it was LaLa sucking my dick and my nut rose quick as hell. I pulled out and busted all on the hoe's face even getting some of my cum in her weave. Shit that's what she get for trying to take my nut.

"'Preciate it ma."

I pulled up my pants and zipped them up before turning around to leave. The bitch had a surprised look on her face. Like what she thought we were going to fuck or she was going to get something other than a nut from me? I didn't ask her to suck my dick, she did that shit all on her own. I left up out of the store without buying anything. I didn't consider getting my dick sucked cheating and wasn't worried about it since my dick wasn't smelling like another bitch's pussy. To me it wasn't disrespectful to my lady at home.

When I stepped into the house I instantly smelled some food that smelled good as hell. I hadn't eaten since breakfast so my stomach was empty as fuck. I walked over to the kitchen and saw Larissa dancing around the room with her back to me as she was stirring a pot on the stove. She had some Beyoncé playing and was wearing one of my T-shirts. I knew she had nothing on under it.

"This the shit I like to see. My woman taking care of her man. What you cooking?"

"Just some stewed chicken, rice, and cornbread. I was hungry and came down here to see what you had to eat. You actually got a lot of stuff in here. I was surprised."

"I gotta eat shorty. I cook a little bit. Most of the time the food just goes to waste I'm not gonna lie."

"Well sit down and I'll bring you your plate in a minute. I know you're hungry I can hear your stomach all the way over here."

I came over to where she was standing and moved my hands up under the shirt she was wearing. I wrapped my arm around her from behind and stuck my finger in her pussy that was already wet like I knew it would be. I fucked her with my hand for a minute, then pulled it out and licked her juices off my fingers. Her pussy was tight like I left that shit too making me glad I had locked her ass down before I left.

"Your pussy gonna be my dessert. Shit sweet as fuck."

I left her standing there knowing she was ready to jump on my dick. I could fuck that girl any and everywhere, but wanted her to be begging for it tonight so I let her go this time.

After placing all the bags inside that were in my car, I kicked my shoes off and went into the living room where I turned on my wall to wall flat screen TV. I flipped through the channels until I found the news like I usually did to keep up with the crazy shit going on in the world.

LaLa brought me a plate filled with food and some juice to drink. I tore that shit up. Damn this girl could cook too. I was a lucky ass nigga to have found her ass. I sat my plate down on the table and looked over at Larissa.

"So I know you going to school and about to graduate soon, but you're gonna be staying with me. You already eighteen and grown so there's nothing stopping you. I need you here with me La. You gotta nigga open." I let her know.

"I'm down but if shit go south with us I'm telling you right now we're not going to be together Messiah. I'm not a dumb girl out here. I expect loyalty and honesty remember that shit. I'll stick with you until the end if you keep it real. If not, I'm out of here like I never knew you"

"You're with a real ass nigga, I got you for real. You just gotta trust that I'm in this shit."

I picked her ass up and carried her upstairs with her legs wrapped around me. We were kissing and I started playing with her nipples. Once inside my room I told her to take the shirt off. I went and sat down in the chair I had against the wall, on the side of my California King bed.

"Go fix me a drink at the table over there. I want to see your sexy ass cater to your man."

LaLa went over to the table where I kept my liquor. She poured me a shot of D'usse and brought it right over to me. She was obedient and did that shit exactly like I told her with a sexy walk and smile. Her titties and ass were bouncing with each step and I couldn't wait to touch, lick, and suck every inch of her golden skin. She was bad as fuck and all mine. My dick was ready to bust out of my pants at the sight of her perfect body.

"Anything else daddy?

She said while making eye contact. Eye contact was some shit that always turned me on. I liked to see the expression a woman had when I was fucking them.

"Get over on the bed and bust that pretty pussy wide open for daddy. I want to see you play in it while I watch that shit."

She walked slowly over to the bed. I pulled my pants and shirt off then sat back down in the chair sipping on my drink. Larissa laid down at the edge of the bed and put each of her feet on the sides. Her legs were spread wide as fuck. She was flexible as hell. LaLa continued to look into my eyes as she took her finger and started rubbing on her clit in circular motions. She began squeezing and playing with her nipples with her free hand. Her moans were getting louder and I began to stroke my dick while I watched her.

"You like that Messiah? You like the way my pussy's wet for you?" Larissa asked.

She put another finger in her pussy and began moving her hand faster. I was stroking my dick nice and slow while I enjoyed the view of her fat pussy only a few feet away. She used her thumb to rub her clit. Moving it fast as hell while dipping her other fingers in and out of her opening. I matched her pace with the strokes of my hand while finishing my drink.

Her free hand kept rubbing her titties and playing with her nipples until she had made herself cum. Then she brought her fingers up to her lips and sucked on each one still keeping eye contact with me. That shit turned me on even more because I loved the way her pussy tasted.

"You like what you see Messiah?" LaLa repeated in a sexy ass voice.

"I love that shit LaLa. You ready for me?" I asked and she nodded her head yes.

I put my glass down and came over to the edge of the bed and got down so her pussy was in my face. I grabbed both of her outstretched legs and put them over my shoulders. I lifted her ass up gripping it tight as hell and went to work eating her pussy for dessert. I vibrated my tongue while I sucked hard on her clit with her ass in the air. I felt her shaking and all her juices squirted out into my mouth. I drank that shit up, before letting her ass back down on the bed and kissing her deep. I wanted her to taste the shit too.

My dick was hard as fuck and I couldn't wait another minute to be inside her. So I stood up and buried my dick all the way in her pussy. LaLa's pussy was slippery wet and let a nigga right in before her tight walls clamped down on my shit. I knew it had been a minute since she had the monster dick in her life so she was screaming out and putting scratches in my back. That made me go harder.

I picked her legs back up and started beating the pussy up and making her take the dick.

"Messiah, fuck me harder. Yes!"

I fucked her harder just like she wanted and with each stroke her pussy got tighter and tighter on my dick. Her ass started trying to back up and run from the dick because I was in so fucking deep, but I wasn't having that shit either.

"You gotta take this mothafucka LaLa. Stop running girl."

I gave her even deeper strokes and felt her body tense up while she was cumming. I let that shit go and busted while she was screaming my name at the top of her lungs.

Her pussy was enough for me I realized at that moment. I wasn't trying to lose this girl over some dumb bitch I was fucking on the side. I made the decision at that moment to try and do right by her and stop fucking around. She deserved a nigga who was gonna be down for only her. I just hoped I could be that man because I couldn't lose her.

Larissa

Over the past few months I had been happier than I ever thought possible. Messiah came into my life and completely turned shit around. I loved that man and he was my world even if he didn't realize it yet. My feelings ran deep for that nigga but I still kept focused on school. Deep down inside I knew shit could switch up in a heartbeat, and people could too. I wanted to fully trust Messiah and completely let him in but I just wasn't there yet. We fell into a comfortable routine these past three months and really had a good thing going on.

I couldn't shake the bad feeling in the pit of my stomach. It was like I was waiting for the other shoe to drop and for him to let me down. I recognized that it probably had more to do with how my parents fucked me over and nothing to do with Messiah. So I tried to set my unease aside and only think positive shit.

Graduation was right around the corner and I had already been accepted to the University of Wilmington where I planned to attend in the fall. I was accepted to a few other colleges out of state too but I wanted to stay near Messiah. If it wasn't for Messiah I wouldn't even have had the money for the application fees or food to eat these past few months. He stepped up and was there for me when my own mother didn't give a fuck. I was going to do everything I could to make our relationship work as long as he continued to be the man he promised to be. It wasn't that I felt obligated to him, I was just happy with him.

Me and Shanice wanted to go out tonight to celebrate our graduation which was tomorrow. We hadn't had a girl's night since the time when me and Messiah first got together, so it was way past due.

Since getting together with Messiah my life had been upgraded. I didn't ask for any of the shit he bought me and felt like he did way too much for me as it was. But he wasn't trying to hear it though. My closet was filled with Michael Kors purses, Gucci, Giuseppe, Versace, you name it. None of the designer clothes or material shit really mattered to me but he always was telling me as his woman I had to carry myself a certain way. So I began to wear the name brands and was getting used to what it meant to be with a boss like him.

Messiah spoiled me and always treated me with respect. He would even take me with him all over town and make sure everyone knew I was his woman. I came to realize that he wasn't a regular dope boy out here. He really was a boss nigga like he always told me. Even when we went to dinner I would catch both men and women staring at him. Some would come over and speak, always showing respect when talking to him. It was to the point that when I went places without him people would show me a certain level of respect too. I guess because they feared what Messiah would do if they didn't.

There was plenty of groupie bitches that stayed lurking around too it seemed. The bitches would give me evil ass looks or try to be slick and find a way to disrespect me. I couldn't count the number of times some hoe tried to make a pass at Messiah trying to fuck him with me right there. He always put them in their place and got them out of his face. He would even force them to apologize to me. He never gave me a reason to worry when it came to being down for me. Everything he promised to be he lived up to so far.

It was like we were hood royalty and although I was getting used to all that came with being with him, sometimes I wished things could be simpler. I was falling in love with Messiah and didn't want to think about life without him. So I was trying to be the woman he needed by his side but it wasn't easy.

There had been a change in my man over the past few months as well. I could tell he was falling for me and trying to do right by me. But he also was gone a lot of the time. He would spend most nights at home with me but about once a week he would stay gone all night. I knew he was branching out and trying to put together an enterprise while having the whole state on lock with the drug game so I understood why he was gone so much.

He still kept most of his business dealings away from me. He said that he didn't want to get me caught up in some shit so it was to best to keep it that way. I wanted to be a part of his life and somebody he could count on so I wished he would confide in me more and let me be a listening ear when he was stressed out. His operation was a big part of who he was and it felt like he was not only holding back his lifestyle from me, but a part of himself. I knew for us to really work he was gonna have to open up to me completely.

I also couldn't stand when he didn't come home or answer his phone. To me it wasn't that hard to send a text or communicate something to me. I didn't want to put up with shit like that and I let his ass know I wouldn't be tolerating it forever. That was really the only problem we had since being together. Our personalities complemented each other well and overall life was really good right now.

Messiah and I would spend hours laid up talking about random shit. He also made me feel secure and protected. Honestly he treated me like a queen and with me moving in everything between us just got better. Nothing was forced or hard between us. He pushed me to finish school and stay focused too. I thanked God every day for allowing Messiah to be a part of my life and I hoped he felt the same about me.

I called up my best friend and told her to come over so we could get ready for our night out together. Once she arrived we started fixing ourselves up. She did my hair and makeup and I did hers. Tonight I put two braids in her hair with a part down the middle. We were going to a regular club. Not some fancy shit like last time so we weren't going to be wearing dresses.

She had on some little ass high waist jean shorts with a red crop top. On her feet were a pair of black booties with open toes. Her skin was glowing and she looked amazing. I picked out some black leather pants that were skin tight and a sheer black top that had a gold bustier underneath to wear. I also wore gold strappy pumps to finish the look. Shanice straightened my hair and now it was sitting just above my ass. We were some fly ass bitches and I couldn't wait to see the heads turn tonight.

Before we left I tried to call Messiah one last time. I hadn't spoken to him since yesterday and was worried that something happened to him. Which was another reason I couldn't handle not being able to contact his ass. I was left out here not knowing what might have happened to the man I loved. Since he was out in the streets there was no telling what could happen to him. I decided I was done trying to call him for the night and turned my phone off before stashing it in my purse. Fuck it! If he didn't care about me being able to contact him then why should I? On the ride over we smoked a blunt and got hyped for the night.

"Where's Money at bitch? He know you left the house looking like that?" Shanice asked as we rode downtown to the club.

"Fuck Money. He don't want to answer the phone so he don't need to worry about shit I do." I said with more certainty than I felt.

It hurt to know this man was probably out there not thinking about me. If he was thinking about me he could at least answer. I mean damn it's not hard to pick up a phone. I never nag him, so there's no reason to avoid me.

"Okay girl, don't get fucked up though. You know who your nigga is right?" she busted out laughing like the shit was funny.

"I'm just trying to turn up with my best friend tonight. I'm not worrying about him!"

"I know that's right." She yelled as we parked.

We walked down the block to where the club was located. When we got to the front we noticed a line out front but we weren't about to stand in a damn line. Shanice led the way up to the front of the cut line and told them I was Money's woman. The men looked at me and must have recognized me from the times me and Money went out around town. We never went to the club but he took me everywhere else with him. When he made time for me that is.

I saw all the hate on the bitches faces as we walked past and the appreciation from their niggas as they looked our way. We were bad as fuck and about to show out up in here. Since I was money's woman I got special treatment and they showed us to a VIP section. We didn't even need to go out on the dance floor. Me and Shanice had bottle after bottle of wine sent over to us and danced in our section the whole night. When the

109

club's lights came on it was only around two in the morning and we weren't ready to go home yet. We were feeling good but not sloppy drunk. Shanice talked me into going to the strip club because we both had never been. She knew about one a few blocks over we could walk to called Mack City that her cousin owned.

The walk over to the club was even fun as hell. There was all kinds of people out at this time of night walking from bar to bar and being rowdy as hell. We made our way to the spot in no time. We didn't have to pay the cover since we were females. So we walked right in over to the side of the stage where there was two empty seats.

The place was pretty packed and there was a stripper on stage who had Asian looking eyes and a crazy ass body. She was working the pole and then dropped down into a split. She spotted us and crawled over to where we were. When she made it to the edge of the stage she opened her legs for us to get a full view of her pussy, and I have to admit the shit turned me on. She had a pretty pussy to be a stripper and it looked tight too. She turned around and started putting her ass right in my face. Then turned around and told me I could touch.

She nodded over to the bouncer and I started rubbing on her fat ass. It must have been the drinks and the fact I hadn't seen Messiah all day and was horny as hell. I slapped her ass a few times while Shanice let singles she got from the bar rain down on her. She ended her set and made her way off stage while Shanice and I just sat back and continued to enjoy ourselves. We watched a few more strippers do their thing on stage. I could never be a stripper but I tried not to judge others and some of them were really pretty girls.

After a few drinks I knew it was time to stop so I wouldn't get too drunk. I finally let my gaze wander away from the stage to take note of the entire club. It was nice considering it was a strip club. I told Shanice I needed to use the restroom so we both got up to go. We never went alone anywhere that's how bitches got you. We walked down the hallway lit with red lights and found the bathroom.

When we got inside I went directly into the stall. I heard noises coming from the stall next to me like a couple was fucking. Whoever was over there fucking was doing a damn good job too. They were banging on the stall hard as hell and I wouldn't be surprised if they broke the shit. The man was definitely putting it down from the moans and screams coming from the girl. I tried not to laugh as I washed my hands.

"Take the dick ma."

I heard from a familiar voice as I finished. I couldn't figure out where I had heard that voice before. Shanice was staring at the stall with a look of disgust on her face. It was crazy to think someone would just come fuck in the stall at a strip club but who was I to judge. It probably was some stripper making some money on the side or something. At least they were enjoying it anyway. I wish I was getting some dick from Messiah but his ass couldn't even answer the damn phone for me.

"Shit Money I'm about to come daddy."

Did that bitch just say Money? Like MY man? Those words caught my attention right away. My heart started racing and my body started shaking. I immediately kicked the stall in and saw some shit nobody should have to see. I saw my nigga, the man I loved fucking that same Asian stripper from earlier in a gotdamn bathroom stall.

My heart broke as I realized what the fuck I had walked in on. When I looked down at his dick the nasty mothafucka didn't even have a condom on. I couldn't take this shit, it was too much for me. All I had done was love Messiah and he hurt me in the worst way. He lied to me every day looking in my face making me believe I was the only one he wanted. Obviously he had been playing my ass the whole time.

I didn't even waste my breath. I knew I couldn't control the tears that were pouring down my face but I wasn't gonna let Messiah break me down even further. He looked like he knew he fucked up when he saw me but there wasn't anything he could do to fix this shit. I caught him with my own eyes and there was no going back. We made eye contact for a brief second before I turned to leave. He tried to grab my arm with his dick still out and all.

"Don't fucking touch me nigga. This shit is over." I yelled as I pulled away out of his grasp.

"No the fuck it's not. You not leaving me. I love you LaLa!" He yelled right back.

I started laughing like a crazy person and kept walking. This nigga had his dick wet with another bitch's pussy juices talking about he loves me. I didn't want that kind of love so he could keep it. Fuck him was all I could think and I was serious about us being over. I didn't do that dumb for love type shit. No matter how much I loved him I loved myself more and I deserved better than how he had done me.

Messiah (Money)

I had been heavier in the streets over the past few months than ever before. Everything went according to plan with the takeover of the state. My connect Fe was impressed when I called him after only a month and told him we were ready to settle up. Once we had our sit down, we established some better terms.

I increased the amount I was getting by having a shipment come in twice a month. The prices would be the same but now I could pay upfront and not worry about having to pay shit back. Fe let me know that his boss was also very impressed and promised a sit down in the near future. Our entire team across NC was some mothafuckin' hustlers and everybody who was down with us was eating good since the takeover.

We opened up more traps in each of the cities too. Any dope sold in the state of North Carolina was being supplied by our new empire, Money Makers Inc. We also started getting some heroin and pills in with our regular dope shipments to expand our operation even more.

On the business front shit was going smooth as hell too. I busted my ass finding a team of the right mothafuckas to bring into the business. We rented out a building downtown to work out of. As of right now, we had an assistant that worked under me, Draco and Silk. We hired two accountants that were top of the line when it came to making shit happen with our investments. We had a sales and marketing crew too to keep up with the latest trends of the market.

Every decision still came through me before any moves were made with both the legal and illegal shit we had going on. We already purchased three businesses that were on the brink of filing bankruptcy to fix up and wash our money with. Now our drug money was being turned into legal money before we sent it off to our banks in the States and our off shore accounts. We weren't taking any chances with losing our bread if the feds ever figured shit out.

My home life had been damn near perfect too. Me and LaLa were still going strong and there wasn't shit I wouldn't do for that girl. She came into my life when I wasn't looking for a woman and wasn't ready to settle down. But she changed my whole outlook on that shit. She was gonna be my wife one day. She had my heart, but I still hadn't told her I loved her.

That was until tonight when she caught me and Chyna fucking. Larissa was everything I wanted in a woman. She was sexy and had ambition. I knew I was living wrong for continuing to fuck around on her. I tried to stop that shit but over the past month I fucked up more times than I could count.

I fell back into my old habits and fucked around on her with both Carina and Chyna from time to time. I hadn't fucked around with no new bitches though, but temptation was a mothafucka and they were always throwing the pussy at me too. I didn't know if I was even cut out for that monogamy shit.

I really fucked up tonight and was reckless with my shit. I came out to the strip club because I was trying to avoid going home for a little while longer. I had been laid up with Carina for the past day handling shit for the baby. Carina was due any day now and I waited to buy anything until yesterday when I finally came to terms with the fact I was about to be a damn father. Carina was having a little girl.

I just wish it was LaLa having my child instead of Carina's ass. I really couldn't see me having kids with any woman beside Larissa. But I had to face facts and accept my responsibility.

I knew LaLa was mad about me being gone but more because I wasn't answering her calls. I hated to see the worry and concern she showed my ass especially when I didn't deserve that shit. She had called me a few times and I ignored her each time.

The thing about Larissa was she really didn't talk shit about my lifestyle or the long hours I was gone. She didn't say shit about anything other than not answering or calling once in a while. She was fucking perfect and now I had fucked around and probably lost her for good.

I was also avoiding going home because I made up my mind to tell Larissa about the baby. I needed to clear my head and get up the courage before I laid shit out in the open. I wasn't no bitch by any means but I knew the shit was going to hurt LaLa and that was the last fucking thing I wanted to do.

She didn't do shit to deserve me having baby on her even if we wasn't together yet when it happened. I knew that she was gonna feel some type of way and I couldn't blame her because I didn't want anyone other than her to have my seeds either.

Chyna hit me up asking me to stop through so we could catch up. I knew what she really wanted was some dick and the best way to clear my mind was to bust a nut. I left Draco and Silk at the spot downtown after playing cards, drinking and smoking the night away. I wanted to forget about the dilemma I was in so I put back a bottle and smoked more than usual before I even made it to Mack City to meet up with Chyna.

When I got to the club Chyna spotted me as soon as I walked through the door. Her ass and titties were out from just finishing her set. She knew I liked public shit and I was ready to fuck the minute I saw her. While she led me down the hall I pushed her up against the wall and used my fingers to play in her pussy right there where everybody could watch that shit. I let her pull me into a bathroom stall after that.

Chyna was a stripper and I treated her ass accordingly but the fact that she didn't fuck with no other niggas who came to Mack's made me do shit like this with her to prove a point more than anything. I was a boss ass nigga and I was the only nigga who could do whatever the fuck I wanted with Chyna and her pussy anytime I wanted. All these other niggas was wishing they were me already. Then to come in here and fuck the bitch they spent racks on and fantasized about made it that much better for me. I was a greedy ass nigga and wanted it all. I wanted my fucking wife who was better than all these other bitches out here and I wanted the benefits of pussy on the side.

I was fucking Chyna giving her some of this dope dick in the bathroom stall about to bust when the stall door got kicked in. Before I knew what the fuck was happening I was face to face with the woman I loved. I swear I saw her damn heart breaking right in front of my eyes and there wasn't shit I could do to make it better. There wasn't no talking my way out of it or making it right either.

I sobered up quick as hell and realized I had more than fucked up. Not only was I caught fucking another bitch. I was caught with a stripper and was fucking her raw. I couldn't do shit but watch as LaLa walked away. I tried to hurry the fuck up and get myself together to go after her as soon as she said that it was over between us. I knew Larissa didn't deserve none of this shit but I wasn't trying to let her leave my ass no matter what. I couldn't lose her.

"Oh so that sexy bitch is yours huh? Shit I want to fuck her too. I bet her pussy is bomb and she seem like a freak. We should all hook up sometime. She's a pretty bitch Money."

Chyna said without realizing she even fucked up with the shit that came out of her mouth. I turned around and wrapped my hand around Chyna's throat.

"Shut the fuck up! Don't say a word about my damn wife. I'm not fucking with your ass no more so don't hit my line again!"

I was mad as hell. I didn't even want to think about the shit Chyna was saying because Larissa was all mine. Not even another bitch could have her and Chyna just reminded me how much I really fucked up.

I was the one who made the decision to come up here and fuck with her. I continued fucking around on LaLa after we made shit official between us. If I lost her it would be on me no one else.

"Whatever nigga, you'll be back. You know you love my pussy. You can't stay away, and if I see your girl I'll let you know." She hollered back while walking away.

I continued on my way and hurried up to get the fuck on. I knew I needed to rush home to see if I could keep LaLa from leaving me. The thought alone had me doing over 90 downtown driving like a crazy ass nigga.

When I got home all the lights were off. I rushed inside and started calling Larissa's name. I searched through the entire house and finally made my way upstairs to our bedroom. I saw the closet light on and when I went over to the door I realized she took all of

117

her regular school clothes and shit with her. She left the rest of the designer dresses, shoes and bags I had bought her. I went over to bed and sat down to catch my breath and noticed a note was on top of one of the pillows.

Messiah,

I gave you a chance. I opened up. I trusted you. I loved you. Tonight you showed me how much I mean to you. You broke my heart. Good luck in life. I'm done. If you see me again pretend you don't know me and I'll do the same.

Larissa

I read it over and over again. The more I thought about the shit I'd been doing to LaLa, the more I realized how bad I fucked up. I had done all the shit I told her I wouldn't. I didn't have her back like I said I would. I really lost the one person who I needed most.

Shanice

It was the end of July and hot as shit outside. I was ready for August to get here so me and Larissa could leave this damn city. We both needed a fresh start and going away to college would give us that opportunity. We were accepted to the University of South Carolina. At first neither of us were going to go there. But when Money fucked up and cheated on her that changed. I wanted to get away from my parents and stay close to my best friend. So needless to say, we both changed our minds and would be leaving for South Carolina at the end of the summer. We figured we would be better off going to school at the same place and away from here.

Larissa was staying at my house since the week of graduation and the night we caught that dog ass nigga fucking that stripper bitch. My parents were fine with her staying here since they were hardly home and liked the fact that I would be home more with Larissa being here.

They were hoping it would keep me out of the hood. Little did they know I still went to the hood on the regular, I just brought Larissa with me. We made sure to stay the fuck away from places we could possibly see her ex at which was fine with me, because it meant I wouldn't have to see that fuck nigga Silk either.

I still thought about him from time to time and saw him around sometimes. He always tried to speak to me but I would just walk away. I wish his ass wasn't so sexy. It's like every man I've met since talking to him I compare to him without meaning to.

Larissa and me were getting everything ready for when we left next month. We hadn't decided our majors yet but figured we could decide sometime during our first semester. We planned on living off campus and having an apartment close to all the local spots in town. My parents were happy that I was even going to college, so they were fine with footing the bill and I damn sure wasn't about to complain.

"LaLa, girl you got to eat something."

I tried to convince her to eat the bowl of soup I had brought up from the kitchen.

"I can't eat nothing girl. I keep throwing everything up." she said weakly.

"Well if you're not better by tomorrow I'm taking your ass to the doctor's. You've been sick for the past three days."

"Okay, but I'm fine I just need to sleep it off. I'm going to lay back down."

As Larissa laid back down I left out of her room and went back downstairs. Since she was out of it for the day I guess I would go see what was going on in the hood. I picked up my keys and headed out the door.

Once I was on the east side near my cousin's house I parked on the curb like usual and jumped out of my car. I loved my jeep and couldn't nobody tell me my ride wasn't the shit. Since it was hot as hell today I was wearing a white romper with a pair of Keds. Something to stay cool in and look cute in too.

I walked past my cousin Brian and one of his friends that was out on the stoop with him. I had never seen his friend before and I noticed he was fine as hell. He was staring at me, basically eye fucking me while I passed. I didn't mind though because he looked like my type and I hadn't messed with a nigga in over a year so I was way past due for some attention. The nigga came up to me and stood in the way before I could enter the house.

"How you doing beautiful. I couldn't help but stop you and see what's up with you. What's your name shorty?"

He stood about a whole foot taller than me. I had to look up and see if he was just as sexy up close. The nigga was turning me on already with his light complexion and sexy eyes. He had a strong build that had me wanting to see what he was working with under his clothes. I placed my hand on his forearm which was strong as hell and smiled at him.

"I'm Shanice, it's nice to meet you. I've never seen you around here before."

"I just came up from Miami. I'm handling some business and will be in town for a minute. Let me get your number so I can take you out."

I figured what the hell maybe one fling before heading off for college would be a good idea. I needed some dick in my life even if I wasn't ready for anything serious. Hopefully I wasn't wasting my time on this nigga. I would get his name, give him my number and then it was up to him from there. Even though I wanted some dick I wasn't about to be a hoe. He still had to work for it and then if he was worthy I would happily give it up.

"Alright give me your phone, and what's your name?" I asked.

"Torio." He said with a deep voice as he handed me his phone.

I was enjoying his company already. It seemed like we had a pretty good connection just from the few words we exchanged.

"Make sure you use it."

I gave his phone back and went ahead and made my way inside the house. I sat around smoking and catching up for a few hours with my cousin. Nothing new was going on in the hood except for the nigga Torio being in town. Bitches were already flocking to him from what Mercy was telling me. I made sure to tell her about our encounter so word would get out. I wasn't trying to claim that nigga or anything. I just wanted to be petty and have the bitches more mad at me than usual because they always thought they were doing something when they weren't.

After pulling my car into the driveway I saw I had an unread message. I opened up the message which was from that nigga Torio already.

"Glad I met you today sexy. I'm taking you to lunch tomorrow."

I chose not to respond tonight. I didn't want to seem thirsty. He definitely was my type of nigga though. He didn't wait to be told yes or no by me and instead took charge. I would see if it fit in my schedule and let him know tomorrow if I was available. Just because he told me, didn't mean I would obey. I liked to give a man a challenge.

Larissa

The morning light was shining through the bedroom I was staying in waking me up from my sleep. The last few weeks had been hard on me and I kept to myself for the most part since the breakup with Money. He had broken me all the way down.

I was doing just fine before I met him. Then he came into my life and I gave his ass a chance. I knew better than anyone how people could fuck you over. Loyalty was rare and I shouldn't have been surprised that Messiah did the shit he did to me. I felt like it was my fault to think he was different in the first place. I should have never opened up to him.

I was glad to have met him and the sex was amazing so I wouldn't take back the time we spent together for nothing. I just wish I had protected my heart better. I should have known he wasn't shit, and everything he was telling me was bullshit. I fell for everything he told me, like a fool even though I knew better.

Shanice proved to me that she was a real friend. She talked her parents into letting me stay here until we went away to college. I was planning to stay local, but now I just needed to get as far away as possible. Everything about this city reminded me of Messiah's ass. I was trying my best to move on and not think about him anymore. But it seemed like he always stayed on my mind. I would catch myself thinking about what he was doing or how he was since we broke things off. I needed to get away and forget about him altogether.

When we were living together it felt so right and we never really had arguments or problems. So I couldn't understand why I wasn't enough for him. One thing I did know how to do was move on though. I learned a long time ago to suck shit up and keep moving forward in life no matter how people fucked you over.

I never would let someone see me down. I managed to steer clear of Messiah so far by avoiding all the places I knew he went to often. I figured I would see him eventually. But the longer I had to get over him the stronger I could be when we came face to face again. I knew with time it would get easier and I could find some happiness again. I wasn't planning on trying to find another man. I honestly thought Messiah and me were meant for each other and didn't see me opening up to another nigga anytime soon.

The past few days I had been sick as hell. I couldn't keep any food down and was only able to drink water. All I wanted to do was sleep. I was worried that something was really wrong with me, or the other possibility was that I was pregnant.

Messiah and I had unprotected sex from the time we met. I mentioned getting on birth control but he didn't believe in it and thought it would mess up my body. He said there was no way he was wearing a condom with me or pulling out either. I went along with the shit and thought if it was meant to be and I got pregnant then so be it. That was when I was dumb and believed we had a real relationship though. If I was pregnant I didn't know if I would keep it or not. It would be something I would decide if I was in fact pregnant.

When Shanice left yesterday I went ahead and called an OBGYN's office to make an appointment. I thought that I would check on the pregnancy possibility first. Then if I wasn't I would go to a regular doctor to see what the hell was going on with my body.

As I laid in bed I realized how much better I was feeling and almost called to cancel my appointment. But decided it was best just to go ahead and find out for sure. I walked downstairs and found Neesy in the kitchen fixing a bowl of cereal. My stomach was growling and the cereal looked good as hell. I went over and fixed a bowl for myself and then sat down next to my best friend.

"Do you mind coming with me to the doctor's in a little while?" I asked her.

"Of course I don't mind bitch. What time? And I see you're feeling better." She replied as she looked over at me eating the cereal.

"It's at ten. Yeah I can finally eat." I said between bites.

After breakfast we both got ready and then headed out to my doctor's appointment. I kept the real reason for the appointment to myself until we pulled into the parking lot at the doctor's office. Shanice figured out why we were really there. She looked over at me.

"So you might be pregnant? That's why we're at an OBGYN doctor right?"

I nodded my head. I wasn't ready to talk about the possibility yet. The thought of being pregnant was scaring me to death.

"Alright well let's go see if I'm about to be an aunt." She said with all the excitement I wasn't feeling at all.

Once inside I signed in and sat down in the waiting area next to Shanice. There was only one other couple in the waiting room and they were just now being called back. A nurse opened the door to the back and called my name so I got up ready to follow her. Shanice stood up and began walking with me. I was so grateful to have a friend like her in my life.

While we were in the hallway walking to the room we passed the payment counter. I happened to look over and saw some more shit that I didn't wanna see. There Messiah stood next to some bitch I had never seen before.

The bitch looked like she was about to fucking pop. She had to be due any day now. I stopped walking altogether and was stuck staring at the two of them without even realizing it. Money looked over and his eyes met with mine for a moment. He instantly dropped his arm from around the woman. But he wasn't mine anymore so there was no reason for him to try and hide the shit he was doing.

Shanice walked back over to me once she realized I wasn't following the nurse anymore. She immediately saw the reason why I stopped and she gave him a death stare. Then said quietly to me.

"That nigga ain't shit. Let's go. Don't let him see you hurt baby girl."

I turned my head and kept walking towards the room the nurse led us to. Shanice was absolutely right. I didn't shed not one tear for that nigga or the shit I just witnessed. He wasn't a part of my life anymore. Seeing him alone would have been hard on me but seeing him with a pregnant bitch hurt me even more.

It was like a knife to the fucking heart. But I had to move on. I couldn't love a man who didn't love me the way I deserved. I wished my heart would just let him go completely so I didn't have to feel any pain behind his actions. I could only hope with time it would get better.

The doctor confirmed that I was pregnant. Two months to be exact. We got to hear the heartbeat and as soon as I heard the life growing inside me, I knew there was no way I could kill my baby. I didn't care if Money and I were together or not, or whether he was even a part of our child's life. I would be responsible for this baby and be the best mother I could be.

On the way home Shanice and I talked about how we were still gonna go away to college. Since my due date wasn't until after the first semester I would just take second semester off. It seemed like having a baby really could work and with her help I knew my child would be fine. As soon as we settled in at school I was planning to get a job to help pay bills anyway. Things were looking up for me and seeing Messiah wasn't about to fuck it up.

Carina

That stupid bitch saw me with my baby daddy at the doctor's office today. I caught her staring at him and saw how sad she looked. She was about to cry. But fuck her and whatever she thought they had. I almost laughed when I saw her ass. I held that shit in because I knew Money had some feelings for the bitch and would flip the fuck out if I was disrespectful.

The shit was funny as hell to me because she had no fucking clue he had a whole family out here while she was playing house with his ass. She was getting everything she deserved for messing with my nigga.

I was due to have my baby yesterday but since she didn't come yet the doctor scheduled me for a C-section tomorrow. I was so ready to get this baby out of me. Don't get me wrong, I knew this baby was my ticket to a better life, but I hated the whole pregnancy. I wasn't cut out for this shit at all. I was fat and uncomfortable. It was even hard fucking at this point in my pregnancy. I needed my baby to get here so I could get my body and life back.

Money finally stepped up to the plate and started taking care of all my bills. I was getting my hair, nails, and massages at least twice a week. He bought me a townhouse to live in downtown. The place was brand new and he furnished the entire thing. I picked the right nigga to have baby with because he had really come through for me.

I walked into the townhouse with Money following behind me. He stopped right inside the door and tried to leave. I grabbed his dick through his pants and started stroking it. Money could never resist me. I unbuckled his pants and slid them down with his boxers. I wanted to suck his dick so he would be more than ready to dick me down after. I was horny as hell and needed some of his big ass dick.

I got on my knees and began to put his semi hard dick in my mouth. His dick was always hard, so it was strange that he wasn't ready to fuck from the jump. Before I even got my mouth all the way around his shit he pushed my head back and pulled his pants back up. I stayed on my knees and looked up at him with a dirty ass look. Did this nigga just turn down some head from me?

"Carina I'm not fuckin' with you. I'm out. I'll see you tomorrow at the hospital."

He turned around and left like it was nothing. Like I wasn't anything to him. I slowly got back up and walked over to the couch. I found my purse and pulled out my cell phone. I needed some dick and knew exactly the right person to call.

"Can you come over?" I asked one of my new friends.

I hung up once he said he was on the way. If Money didn't want to fuck me there was plenty of niggas who were more than willing. He just didn't realize that I had options too.

Messiah (Money)

I couldn't believe I was caught up in another situation that would hurt Larissa, which was the last thing I wanted to do. She looked good as hell when I saw her at the doctor's office. I saw the hurt in her eyes but also how quick she recovered and let that shit roll off her back. That was my LaLa though she liked to keep her feelings in check and not let others see the pain they caused.

When I spotted her my dick also responded right away. I noticed her tight ass leggings hugging her ass and knew she didn't have any shit on underneath. I also saw her hard nipples through the tank top she was wearing and all I wanted to do was leave this bitch Carina where she was standing and go get my shorty back.

I tried to respect the fact that she didn't want shit else to do with me. But after seeing her today, I wasn't about to give her any more damn space. I needed her and I wasn't giving up on what we had. She was gonna be mine again end of story.

I wondered why she was at the OBGYN office anyway. I was hoping she was pregnant with my seed. That way she would be stuck with me. Call it what you want but I would be more than happy to trap her ass. I would love to keep her pregnant and have a house full of lil niggas and young queens that took after us. I never strapped up when I fucked her and told her not to take birth control. She would be a good ass mother and I could see that shit now. Thinking she might be pregnant had me smiling for the first time in a long ass time.

Then when I made it to Carina's crib and she tried to suck my dick my mood was instantly fucked up. I had made up my mind to get LaLa back and I couldn't even think about Carina's or any other bitch's pussy. My dick wouldn't cooperate either which never happened to me before. It was time for me to stop fucking around and wife Larissa's ass. I just had to convince her that I was the man for her.

I was riding around town cruising down Main Street when a phone call from Draco came through. So I knew something was up. We usually texted unless it was something important. As soon as I picked the phone up Draco came on the line sounding mad as hell.

"911 Nigga"

"Say less"

I cut the call short and turned the car around. Some shit had gone down and we needed to meet up at the warehouse. We hadn't had no problems since the takeover. It was a smooth transition so there was no telling what the emergency was. If there was a mothafucka dumb enough to fuck with Money Makers Inc. or our drug operation they would be dealt with accordingly.

After the hour drive I pulled into the long driveway leading to the warehouse. I parked my A7 and saw Silk and Draco's whips both were already here. I walked through the doors and the both of them were sitting around the table with a blunt in rotation. Shit had to be bad if they were smoking like this before I got here.

"What's up bruh? I asked as I took my seat at the head of the table.

"One of our traps on the east side got hit." Silk spoke up

"How much they get and who was the mothafucka bold enough to make a move against us in our own city?" I questioned both of them to get an answer.

"We been through all the hoods to see what the word on the street is. But shit's quiet right now. The crews been told to keep their eyes and ears open. We put a reward on this shit."

"How much they get?" I repeated "And how the shit happened in the first place?"

"The dumb nigga who tried to bust the lick only got what was on hand last night. So around fifty g's and a couple keys. Our lieutenant out there got hit but is gonna make it. He was already taken to the hospital when we got there so we didn't get information from his ass yet on what the fuck really went down. Shit's not adding up." Draco said while shaking his head.

I could tell he was ready to murder some niggas for coming against us and I was feeling the same way.

"We got to find the niggas responsible for this shit and send a message. No mothafucka is gonna come against us and live. We make the city bleed until we get the information. Let's go."

We went to grab some extra heat to be prepared for anything that came our way. It was time to let the fuck niggas know who ran this city. We wanted to put an end to the stupid ass niggas responsible for the hit by the end of the night. Niggas was either gonna get out the way or be laid the fuck out.

Me and the boys rode around the rest of the day trying to find out information. We ended up busting a few heads and letting a few off in some niggas that didn't wanna cooperate, but nobody seemed to know shit or they weren't willing to tell us. There wasn't a doubt in my mind that we would get to the bottom of this shit with how much pull we had. We were the fuckin' reason every nigga was eating out here so it was only a matter of time.

We still had the three separate crews working across the city and they had expanded since we made the deal. Now there was at least fifteen niggas working under each lieutenant. I met up with each one, except Brian's ass who got shot in the hit and was still laid up at the hospital.

In his place I promoted my lil nigga who I had been grooming for a while now. The nigga was about his money and a loyal mothafucka who put in work without hesitation. I put the responsibility on each of the crews to find the information, handle the shit, and bring the nigga responsible to us alive.

Being the boss ass niggas we were it was important that mothafuckas in the streets saw that we stayed ready to enforce shit like we did today. They needed to know we would get out there and put in work. That we weren't some weak ass niggas sitting back letting others take care of shit for us. We were the furthest thing from soft or new to this shit.

But at the same time most problems that came up we needed to be able to let the crews handle and trust them to do shit right. If we were ever going to expand further and move into other states we had to limit when we got our hands dirty. I was still going to murder the stupid ass mothafucka who was responsible for the hit. But all the leg work could be handled by our team. Whichever crew handled the situation first was the hungriest and they would rewarded for stepping up and making shit happen.

It was three in the morning and after the crazy ass day I needed some pussy. The only pussy I wanted was

Larissa's though. So I took a chance and dialed her number. I was surprised as hell when she actually answered after a few rings. It sounded like she was sleeping.

"LaLa we need to talk shorty." I spoke into the phone.

"Okay Messiah. It'd be better if we just got this shit over with. You can come pick me up and we can take a ride since I'm awake now."

"Bet" I hung up right away so she couldn't change her mind.

I knew exactly where Larissa was staying. I had gotten her a new phone when we were still living together and that shit had a tracker in it. I wasn't on no stalker shit but I had to make sure she was straight at all times whether we were together or not. She was still mine.

I drove over to the neighborhood her friend Shanice lived in and stopped outside the house. Then I sent a text to let LaLa letting her know I was outside. I was nervous as hell to face her but I had to suck that shit up and do whatever it took to get my baby back. I could admit I was dead ass wrong for the shit I put her through. Now I had to convince her I wasn't about to fuck up a second time if she forgave me.

Larissa walked down the driveway and over to the car like a fucking model. She had on tight ass boy shorts and a T-shirt. She was sexy even just waking up. Damn I loved this girl.

She opened the door and lowered herself into the seat. I wasn't ready to start the conversation yet and didn't want to give her an option of leaving. So I turned the music up and started driving to the spot we had gone to the first night we met. Just being around her in the same car made me feel whole again.

When I put the car in park I turned my head and looked over at LaLa. She was sitting there crying silently. I swear knowing I was the reason she was crying had me feeling like the worst nigga alive. I took my thumb and tried wiping the tears away. I didn't know how to make her feel better so with my other hand I reached in her shorts finding her pussy. I could at least make her body feel good.

I let my fingers slide in her pussy and used my thumb to rub her clit. She was tight as hell and her pussy was leaking. I continued to fuck her pussy with my hand and had her cumming within minutes while tears were still falling from her eyes. Damn I really fucked up. This shit wasn't even helping the situation. I guess it was time to talk.

"LaLa I'm sorry ma. You got my fucking heart. I need you back." I decided to get straight to the point and see how she took what I had to say.

"Really Messiah. That's it? You're sorry? I gave you my heart, I gave you everything and I wasn't enough nigga. What the fuck do you want me to do? Come back home so you can fuck me over again? I can't do that. I got too much going on to think about being with your cheating ass again."

"What you mean you got too much going on LaLa? You fucking another nigga? Let me know what's really up." I started getting mad as hell with the thought of her fucking another nigga when all I wanted was her.

"No nigga. I've never been with anyone else but you. Can't you see all I wanted was you and I wasn't enough for you. You broke my heart and seeing you today, and now tonight, it just hurts."

135

"I'm fucking sorry Larissa. You're more than enough for me. It wasn't nothing you did shorty. That shit is on me. You're my world and I fucked up. I can't take none of the shit I did back but I can guarantee I'll be a better man for you moving forward. I realize how bad I fucked up. I can't stand that I hurt you. Let me prove it to you. Let me be the nigga you want me to be. I can't be out here without you."

"I'm pregnant." She whispered, but I heard her ass loud and clear.

I placed my hand on her stomach even though she wasn't showing and smiled big as hell. It was some fate shit that I had gotten her ass pregnant. Now there wasn't no breaking up or her trying to leave me. I got out of the car and came around to LaLa's side and opened her door. I pulled her hand for her to stand up. Then I closed the car door behind her. This woman was about to have my baby and I wanted to fuck the shit out of her right here, right now. All that other bullshit didn't matter right now.

I began kissing and sucking on her neck and heard her moans in my ear. I lifted her up and sat her down on the hood of my car. As I pulled her shorts off I started placing kisses on her inner thigh while she had her fingers running through my dreads pulling at them. I dove right in like it was my last meal. I was gonna make her want to come back home tonight with my mouth and dick.

I wasn't taking no for an answer. I was eating her pussy while she rode my face. Her body was shaking and I felt her cum. After she let that shit go I licked her clean again and pulled my dick out. She reached up for it and leaned forward kissing the tip before using her hand to guide it into to her pussy. We both watched as she took my entire dick in.

"Fuck me Messiah" She said

"LaLa this your dick. You hear me, it's yours. Look at how your pussy fits my dick."

Her ass was throwing the pussy at me and her shit was wetter than I had ever felt. My nut was rising too fast, so I turned her ass around and entered her again while I bit both of her ass cheeks just enough to leave marks. Then I held her ass cheeks apart so I could watch my dick slide in and out. Each time I gave her a stroke she threw her ass back for me to go deeper.

"Make that ass clap girl. Let me see that shit."

"Fuck Messiah! Yes deeper." Larissa shouted.

I gave her one more deep long stroke and pulled her into me while I busted inside her. My dick was pulsing inside her and I felt her pussy muscles tighten again from the climax she just had. I didn't want to pull my dick out of her and felt like if I did I might not see her ass again. Reluctantly I did since I knew we had to get back in the car and finish the conversation we started.

"I'm bringing you home tonight La." I told her.

Fuck it I wasn't gonna even give her an option.

"Alright Money, but I'm sleeping in the guest room for now. I'm not saying we'll be together. But I'm not gonna lie and say I don't love you either. I'm going away to college next month so hopefully by then we'll have shit figured out between us. At least for the baby."

The last part of what she said caught me off guard because I thought she was staying here for college. To find out she was about to up and leave surprised me. But that shit wasn't happening no matter what she thought. I wasn't letting her leave my side period. I had given her space the last month but I was done letting her think she could leave me.

What we had was the forever type shit and she needed to get with the program. I wasn't gonna ruin the moment though, we still had a lot of problems to deal with. Like the fact that I was supposed to become a father tomorrow. Fuck.

Larissa

I moved back into Messiah's house and had been here for about a week. There wasn't any way I was sleeping back in the master bedroom though and honestly I didn't think our relationship was going to work. But the truth was I loved that nigga with everything in me and walking away was easier said than done. I was still trying to figure out what the hell I was going to do when it came to him.

Now just because we hadn't been sleeping in the same room didn't mean we weren't fucking. We were sexing each other every chance we got, at least two or three times a day. I was horny all the time and couldn't get enough dick. I guess my body was trying to make up for the lost time.

He seemed to be trying to win me back but I kept thinking about what if he switched up again and let me down. I didn't know if he could be faithful. I mean he was fucking that stripper and who knows what other bitches. I'm not dumb so I know he was fucking that girl Carina or should I say his baby mama at least.

That was another thing. I didn't want my man to have a baby by anyone else but me. That may be selfish but I never envisioned my life as a step mom. Carina gave birth to a baby girl the day after I moved back in with Money. He basically dragged my ass to the hospital with him to witness the shit and wouldn't let me leave his side. He was acting clingy as hell this last week not letting me out of his sight. It was like he thought I would leave his ass if he wasn't around. I really was torn between leaving him and giving him another chance at this point.

I had to admit the baby was beautiful. But there was something off and in my opinion she didn't favor Messiah at all. I looked at her every time Messiah and me went to visit her trying to find some similarity between the two and couldn't find none. I talked to him about getting a DNA test and he finally agreed because he said he didn't want to have Carina as a baby mama.

He kept saying how I was the only woman he wanted to have kids with. I knew he already formed a bond with the baby but who knew if the bitch was lying. She looked like a shady hoe to me.

As far as being pregnant, even though I was scared the more I thought about the baby growing inside me the more in love with him I was. I felt that my baby was going to be a boy and I already planned on making him a Jr. Messiah was all about that shit too. I wasn't showing yet but he would constantly find a way to have his hand on my stomach and swore the baby already knew his daddy from how I screamed his name so much while we were fucking. He was stupid as hell about some shit I swear. The shit that came out of his mouth didn't even make sense.

Today I was attending a cookout at Messiah's mother's house. It had been four months since I met Messiah and this was the first time I would be around his family and friends like this. I was nervous to meet his mama and wanted to make a good first impression because I knew how close Messiah was to her.

Every day in the summer down here it was hot as hell so I decided to wear a white sundress with matching white sandals. I also threw my hair up in a high bun to keep it off my neck. After adding the finishing touches to my makeup I grabbed my nude Chanel bag and made my way downstairs to meet Messiah.

He was waiting for me in the living room and when he saw me walking down the stairs he started looking at me like he was ready to fuck. We didn't have time for that if we were going to make it on time and there was no way I was going to be late and have his mama already not liking me.

I grabbed the salad and pound cake I made to bring and started walking out fast as hell. I didn't want Messiah to get nothing started since he was already staring me down. He was so fine I never could resist him. His dark complexion and dreads were perfect to me. I loved to run my hands over his arms and chest which were nothing but muscle. Every time he looked at me it was like he put me in a trance. The things that nigga did to me were indescribable.

"Messiah, will you come get the door? We got to go!" I called to him.

That nigga was still sitting there watching me and now I could see him looking at my ass like he didn't even hear me.

"Messiah we are not about to have sex right now so stop looking at me like that." I said playfully but was serious as hell.

He knew I was nervous about meeting his mama.

"I'll let that shit slide for now but watch how you talk to me. You know I'm a boss ass nigga. Don't play with me. If I want some of MY pussy I'll take that shit."

"Yes daddy," I said only half joking because he was dead ass serious.

He got up and grabbed the dishes out of my hand to carry. So I opened the door and he went ahead and put them into the trunk of the car. The ride to where his family stayed was around thirty minutes. We crossed back into the city limits and I started getting more nervous all of the sudden. Next thing I knew we were getting ready to pull up in front of the house he grew up in. He had showed me the house plenty of times but never brought me until today.

When we stepped out I heard music playing and smelled food cooking on the grill. There were kids playing out front on the sidewalk with water guns like they were at war or something. We walked up the steps hand in hand together and made our way into the house. I saw pictures of Messiah and his brothers on the tables in the living room. I followed Messiah as he led me through the house into the kitchen where his mama was. He sat the cake and salad down and then greeted his mother.

"Mama, I want you to meet Larissa."

"Hey sweetie, I'm Sheila. It's so nice to meet my future daughter in law."

I was caught off guard by her openness, especially since me and her son technically weren't even together right now. I decided to go with it and not give her all the details. I wasn't here for all that and regardless of whether me and Money made it as a couple she would be our baby's grandmother. In fact, the only grandparent that he would have in his life really since I didn't want my parents anywhere near him.

"It's nice to meet you Ms. Lawson." I said with a smile.

"Please call me Sheila. I'm glad Messiah has finally brought you over to meet me. I've heard all about you and been telling this hard headed boy to bring you by. He likes to do things his way. Always has."

I was surprised that Messiah told his mother about me and it made me feel better about being here with him.

"Now go out back and enjoy yourselves. Maurice is out there with some tramp. I can't believe that boy. He knows better than to bring trash up over here."

"Alright ma, you need us to take anything out?" Messiah asked.

"Nope I got it. Now go ahead and relax."

Messiah took my hand and led the way to the backyard where everyone was at. The yard was filled with people. On one side there was a card game going on and then over on the other side some older men were cooking on the grill and frying up some fish. I didn't recognize anyone except for his brother Maurice and Janae who was hanging all over him. Of course the first place we walked was where they were standing with some other people who I assumed were their cousins I had heard about.

"Aye bruh, what you been up to?" Messiah dapped his little brother as he questioned him.

"Nothing you know just ready to finish the year and head out to camp. I've been chilling."

"Let me holla at you for a minute. Come inside real quick"

The two walked back into the house and I was left with this dumb hoe Janae since their cousins had walked away when Messiah and Maurice did.

"So you out here playing the side bitch role with a nigga who got a whole fucking family waiting on him at home I see." Janae said.

"You mean I'm here with my nigga. My baby daddy right?" I rubbed my stomach for emphasis and to be extra petty.

"Whatever bitch! My sister been his main and ain't going nowhere. You just something to do in the meantime."

I don't know what came over me, maybe it was the pregnancy hormones, but I punched that hoe right in the face. She instantly dropped to the ground from the impact of my fist while I stood over her. Usually in a situation like this I would have just walked away instead of fighting unless a bitch touched me first. Janae stood back up and tried to get a hold of me. Before she could touch me though Messiah stepped in and grabbed her arms. He said low but in his deep menacing voice.

"Don't even think about touching her."

He let her arms go and then took ahold of my hand practically dragging me back into the house to what I assumed was his old bedroom. I was too worried about what he was going to do to be embarrassed about how he handled my ass with everybody watching.

He was pacing the bedroom which looked crazy because the room was so small. I sensed how mad he was so I chose to keep my mouth shut until he spoke. Messiah was a dangerous man and I never tried to push him past a certain point. I could tell there was a dark side to him and I didn't want any part of that Messiah.

"The fuck was that Larissa? You out here fighting while carrying my baby. What the fuck is wrong with you?"

"I wasn't fighting. I just punched the bitch. She was disrespectful."

"Oh she was disrespectful huh?"

I waited to say anything else because I was trying to figure out the best way to talk myself out of this and to calm his ass down. What I just told him seemed to make him more mad not help. He was standing still now giving me an evil ass look.

"Bend over that bed."

"What?"

"You heard what the fuck I said Larissa"

He was still mad as hell and yelling at me. Everybody could for sure hear everything he was saying to me. I wasn't a fool so I went over and bent over the damn bed.

"Now I'm about to teach your ass a lesson so you remember who the fuck I am."

I felt him lift my sundress up over my ass and him glide his hand over both my ass cheeks. The sensations were turning me on, but I was also intimidated by how evil his ass sounded.

"Really, you really fucking up!."

Shit I knew he was gonna be really mad now. He hated when I went without wearing panties in public.

"This for doing some shit without thinking."

He came up and whispered in my ear, before he shoved all eleven inches of his dick in me without warning. I swear it felt like my insides were being fucked up. I wanted to scream out so bad but we were in his mama's house so I had to keep it in. He knew what he was doing.

He stayed perfectly still for a minute then pulled his long dick all the way out. He whispered again before taking ahold of my legs.

"This for not having any shit on under your dress."

Then rammed his entire dick back into my pussy. My pussy was throbbing from what he was doing to me. It was like torture and bliss at the same time.

I felt my juices soak the bed underneath me. He had made me cum with two strokes.

"You like this shit huh, LaLa? You like this monster dick teaching you a lesson"

He began going harder and fucking me with no mercy. He moved his arms under me and pinched my nipples from underneath. That had me bucking back against his dick each time he was all the way deep inside my pussy. He lifted my body and had my ass in the air as he continued to fuck the shit out of me. Still I refused to scream out or make a noise for fear of being heard. Having to be quiet was torture in itself but I was loving it too.

"Whose pussy is it LaLa?"

I couldn't say anything without screaming while he was fucking me like he was so I kept my mouth shut. The bed was making so much noise and I felt like his dick was in my stomach. Tears were coming down my face because I couldn't take the dick anymore. My pussy muscles tightened and gripped down to the point that his dick could barely move in and out of me.

"I said who's mothafuckin' pussy is it? He yelled louder.

"Oh my god! It's yours Messiah!"

I finally let out in a scream. As soon as the words came out of my mouth my pussy squirted and his cum filled me up at the same time.

I couldn't believe we just fucked at Messiah's mama house with all those people around. Even though his ass had me crying trying to keep from making a sound while taking the punishment from his dick, I knew the bed had made noise. Plus Ms. Sheila's loud ass son wasn't trying to be quiet at all while fuckin' me good.

I was so embarrassed when we walked out after fixing ourselves back up. Messiah's ass didn't give a fuck. He loved public sex. Ms. Sheila seemed not to notice though and when I went into the kitchen she actually thanked me for giving it to Janae. She said she couldn't stand that girl and she was only trying to use Maurice as her come up. I thought about how her sister and her were so much alike.

Shanice

I missed having my best friend living with me but understood that she had to figure shit out with Money. I saw the love she still had for that nigga and wanted her to be happy even if that meant going back to him. We were leaving for school in three days and we were getting all the shit ready for the move.

Over the past few weeks I had been seeing that nigga Torio. He ended up taking me out a few times. It seemed like he knew all the right things to say because we started fucking around a week after meeting. I hadn't been with a man in so long it felt good to have someone appreciate me.

He was a sexy ass nigga and I loved getting dicked down on the regular. I didn't see anything serious in our future since I was leaving to go away to college. I think he was honestly feeling me more than I was feeling him. But either way once I was gone we could stay in touch and fuck around from time to time.

Tonight Torio was taking me to dinner downtown and then he had a surprise planned afterwards. He really was pulling out all the stops and I loved the attention he was giving me. I wanted to dress sexy but classy tonight so I chose a pink knee length Donna Karen knit dress. It showed off my shape with some cleavage but nothing over the top. My natural hair was blown out and straightened so it was reaching just below my shoulders. I added some lashes and lip gloss for emphasis and was ready to go.

Torio picked me up in his new Mercedes that he bought about three weeks ago just after we met. I knew he was a thug and into the street shit but wasn't exactly sure if it was drugs or what. That wasn't something you came out and asked a nigga when you was riding his dick.

We held hands as we entered the restaurant and were shown to our table by the hostess. We sat across from each other in the back corner booth. It was such a romantic restaurant and the food was delicious.

Torio's whole demeanor changed about halfway through dinner though. His phone kept ringing back to back. It was on vibrate and I told his ass to answer it since he seemed worried about the shit after the first few times it went off. But instead he turned the shit on silent and put it in his pocket. That shit pissed me off to the max. Here he was stressing about who was calling but instead of just answering it he was trying to hide it from me.

I definitely wasn't with the secretive shit, even if we weren't in a real relationship. I was still gonna be respected. There should have been no problem with him answering the damn thing in the first place.

As our plates were being cleared Torio decided to come sit beside me before we ordered dessert so we could look over the menu together. I knew his ass was trying to fix the bad vibes since the phone ordeal. While we were choosing our dessert his hand found my leg and he gripped my thigh before slipping his hand under my dress. I didn't have anything on under the dress because I hardly wore panties which gave him easy access.

He was using his fingers to fuck me slowly right there while no one knew what was happening. I let my anger about being disrespected earlier fade away and began to enjoy the feelings his hand was causing. I closed my eyes and started moving my body in rhythm as he was putting more pressure on my clit before he slid another finger into my pussy. I cummed all over his hand while gripping the table, before opening my eyes back up.

I looked across the room and locked eyes with none other than that nigga Silk. He was staring directly into my eyes and I knew he had been watching me the whole time. His eyes were glazed over with lust and dark with anger. He still had some type of effect on me as well and just to be petty I smiled at his ass. Being sure to keep eye contact with him.

When our dessert arrived Torio moved to his seat across from me and blocked my view of Silk. So I focused back on the nice dinner I was being treated to. This nigga had pulled his phone back out of his pocket though and was texting on it without even touching the dessert we ordered to share. He was glued to the phone and not really paying me any attention.

He must have thought that just by making me cum he could get away with some triphlin' shit. That let me know I needed to stop messing with his disrespectful ass after tonight. I would miss the dick but my feelings weren't involved so it wouldn't be hard to walk away. I wanted to use the bathroom before we left since I didn't know where we were going for the surprise afterwards.

I walked over to the hallway where the bathrooms were and felt a pair of arms pull me from behind. Silk turned me around so that our faces were inches apart.

"So you gonna keep playing with a nigga? When you gonna give me a chance to make shit right?" he asked.

Then he began kissing on my neck while grabbing my ass. Next thing I knew he pulled me into the bathroom and locked the door. He lifted me onto the sink counter and raised my dress up.

"You're gonna be my woman Shanice. You know it so stop fucking around and get with a real nigga."

He released his dick and I was at a loss for words. He had a condom on and had the mothafucka in my pussy before I could stop him even if I wanted to. He spread my legs wider and dug deeper. He was hitting my spot back to back and I clenched my pussy muscles around his dick with every stroke he gave. I started kissing him and sucking on his neck. I was trying to leave a damn mark on this nigga like he was mine. I pulled away and leaned back. I lifted my dress off over my head to give him a better view. Then I began rubbing on my breasts and squeezing my nipples.

"Shit your pussy wet as fuck girl, look at it."

Silk said as he started playing with my clit. All of the sudden he went even deeper and used his hand to pinch my clit hard as hell making me instantly cum all over his dick. The condom was coated with my juices even more. Then he started pounding into me harder and harder until he tensed up and filled up the condom.

"Oh shit! This can't fucking happen again. What the fuck did I do?" I said out loud randomly as I hurried to get myself together.

"Shanice you know this shit was bound to happen. It's time you stop bullshitting around."

"I'm not doing this with you. Forget this shit ever happened." I said while rushing out of the bathroom fast as hell.

I couldn't believe I let shit get that far and while I was on a date with another nigga. This wasn't how I got down at all and the more I thought about it the more ashamed I felt.

When I returned to the table Torio was gone. I mean I was gone probably fifteen minutes but me and Silk only had a quickie. I didn't know where the nigga could have gone. I sat down and decided to wait. Maybe he had an important phone call or had to use the bathroom himself. After waiting twenty minutes and calling his number back to back Torio blocked my number. I realized that nigga really left me here. But I couldn't even blame his ass since he probably thought I took off on his ass too. I hoped he didn't know what I really was up to because that was some foul shit on my part.

I called an Uber and headed home. Tonight had been a crazy ass night, but no matter what Silk thought we had he was sadly mistaken. That ship had sailed. Tonight was an accident, nothing more. I wasn't gonna be stupid for no nigga no matter how good looking, wealthy or how much pull they had over me. It just wasn't happening.

Messiah (Money)

We still hadn't heard a fucking thing from any of our crews about who was responsible for the hit on our spot. That shit was starting to have me rethinking our capabilities as a big time operation. We needed the niggas on our team to get their shit together and find the mothafucka responsible. If one nigga could get away with plotting against us then more would come. We needed to send a message and let everybody know we weren't to be fucked with. The last thing we wanted was for the shit to spiral.

I was in my office at Money Makers Inc. headquarters going over numbers from all our businesses. The shit was easy as hell to turn profits from even without our own money coming into it. Then with the money we were washing on top of it our damn profits were tripling. I was happy as fuck on the business front and our accounts stacking up nicely.

It was time for a trip down to Miami to meet with the connect. Fe wanted me to fly down as soon as possible to discuss some new shit he hoped to add to our current deal. I knew Larissa's ass was trying to leave me in a couple days to go off to college too, but I wasn't letting that shit happen. We hadn't officially gotten back together yet but we weren't apart either. I needed her to stop bullshitting around and forgive me so we could get past the shit I had done. Since having her back home I hadn't even looked at another bitch. The only pussy my dick felt was LaLa's and the shit had me feeling like I didn't want no other bitch at all. I had turned over a new leaf and was ready to be with her one hundred percent.

As I was placing the account spreadsheets back into their folder I saw a text coming through. When I opened it there was a picture message from Chyna of her playing in her pussy. The shit didn't even phase me or get my dick's attention one bit so I erased it and started to put my phone in my pocket when it vibrated again. I looked at the screen and noticed Carina messaged me telling me there was an emergency with Monae.

My life changed so much in a short amount of time. I was a father and the shit felt crazy but I loved that little girl from the moment I first saw her. I hated her damn mother though and every time I was around her I wanted to get rid of the bitch, take my shorty home and have LaLa be her mother instead.

I dragged Larissa with me every time I visited her so Carina wouldn't try no slick shit and so LaLa wouldn't feel no type of way about the situation. LaLa never treated Monae bad or held any spite towards her, but I could see the sadness every time she looked my baby girl in the face. I understood it hurt her for me to have a baby out here that wasn't by her. But now that I was a father I had to put my child first, even before her.

Larissa wanted me to get a DNA test. Even though I felt the baby was mine I was gonna do that shit just to get it settled once and for all. I signed the birth certificate and accepted my responsibility but if the test made LaLa feel better about the whole thing that was the least I could do for her. Plus Carina might have been a no good bitch but she didn't hoe around. I been knowing her for years and never seen her with another nigga.

I hurried up and closed up my office so I could get to Carina's townhouse that I put her up in as fast as I could. This would be the first time I went over there without Larissa but I didn't have time to scoop her ass up first since it was an emergency. I made it there in no time and used my key to let myself in.

When I walked in I saw Carina come out from the back with my daughter crying at the top of her lungs. Carina recovered good as hell from having the C-section. She had a little more pudge in her stomach and her titties were big as hell from breastfeeding. Her ass was even fatter now and for some reason seeing her holding my daughter with only the robe she had on, had my dick hard. My dick hadn't gotten hard from another bitch besides LaLa in a minute. I realized I fucked up coming over here without her.

"What's up with the baby? Why she crying like that?"

"I don't know Money I been trying everything she just won't stop."

Carina walked over to the couch and sat down. She opened her robe and began to breastfeed Monae. I knew Carina was breastfeeding but she hadn't done that shit in front of me before, probably because my girl was always over here with me. I stood there staring at my daughter and baby mama. It seemed like Monae only wanted to be fed so I couldn't understand why Carina didn't do that shit earlier. She was up to something and that shit was affecting my daughter. I wasn't a dumb nigga by no means.

Once Monae was finished eating she fell asleep and Carina laid her in the cradle that was set up out in the living room. She left her robe open so I had a full view of her big titties and fat pussy. Her stomach had a small scar that looked about healed but other than that her body was almost perfect. Her deep brown skin was glowing and she smelled like vanilla or some shit. She stood in front of me and grabbed for my dick through my pants.

"I knew you was hard daddy."

She purred into my ear, before sucking on my neck just how I liked. My dick was trying to get free and she knew that shit. I thought about LaLa and how we fucked earlier before I left for the office. I bet she was at home waiting for a nigga expecting me to be home already to take her greedy ass out to eat. My son growing inside her was a big mothafucka already.

I pulled back away from Carina and put space between us. Shit I wanted to fuck. I couldn't fuck with her though. I wasn't trying to hurt Larissa again and possibly lose her for good when I just got her ass back.

"What the fuck Money?" Carina said nastily.

"You called me over here on some bullshit Carina. I ain't fucking with you period. The only pussy this daddy dick hitting is my lady. You need to get that shit through your head ma."

"So you really gonna pick that bitch over me? After all these years you're gonna tell me that bitch's pussy better than mine? She suck your dick like I do? She ride the dick and take that big ass dick like I do? I don't believe that shit for a second. You know she can't do you like I do nigga."

"You right, she do all that shit better. She's wifey so whatever we had is dead shorty. It's a wrap." I confirmed for her hard headed ass.

"Alright nigga, we'll see when that bitch fuck you over don't come back trying to play house over here."

"I'll let you slide on calling her out her name this time because I know you in your feelings, but I already warned you about disrespecting my girl. I'm out, and don't hit my line with no dumb shit again."

"Fuck you Money! You ain't shit."

I didn't have shit else to say to the scheming ass bitch, so I left without another word. I wasn't a nigga to go back and forth with a bitch. I said what needed to be said and left it at that. She almost got me today with the slick shit she pulled. What kind of mother would lie about an emergency with their baby just to try and fuck? That was some shady ass shit if you ask me.

Larissa

I was in the master bedroom in our home. I say our home because I had decided to give Messiah another chance. He convinced me enough over the past few weeks that he was really trying to be the man he promised to be. Life with him was happier for me than it was without him. I learned that shit during the time we spent apart. So I was really gonna give our relationship another shot.

I walked into the closet and took out a few items that I had never worn. I packed them with everything else I already had in the suitcases. We were leaving for South Carolina in a couple days and I wanted to get everything packed. I was gonna stick to my plan and go away to college. Since it was only a few hours' drive I planned on coming back every weekend to see Messiah. I knew he wasn't wanting me that far away but he hadn't really said much about it the few times I brought it up. So I figured he was trying to avoid it, but would accept my decision.

I folded the clothes into the last suitcase and then zipped it up when I heard footsteps coming upstairs. It was time for us to have a talk about me leaving so I sat on the bed next to the suitcase waiting form Messiah to come into the room. I also wanted to let him know that I was ready to claim his ass again and be in a real relationship with him.

He walked right up to me and stood between my legs. My man was looking stressed the hell out. I took my arms and placed them around his legs then pulled back enough to undo his pants. I knew exactly how to relieve his stress and take his mind off of whatever was bothering him.

I looked at his dick. Of course it was already hard and ready for me. I loved this nigga's dick. It even turned me on just from how good it looked, damn.

"I see this damn monster ready and waiting for me."

"Fuck you mean, your dick stay ready shorty. Now stop playing and show daddy how much you missed me today."

He didn't have to tell my ass me twice. I circled the tip of his dick with my tongue and continued as I worked it all the way into my mouth. I was giving him some sloppy ass head while looking him right in the eyes. He loved that shit. He was staring down at me and had his hand in my hair pulling it just enough to let me know he was in charge. I kept going until he tensed up and I felt his dick jumping. Instead of letting him pull out and fuck me like usual I sucked harder until his cum shot out. I let it slide down my throat and continued to suck until every drop was out.

After giving him some bomb ass head Messiah tried to take my clothes off and finish what I started, but I stopped him. He was always ready to please me and then fuck me senseless. It was like he never got enough and neither did I. But right now I needed to talk to him about some important shit.

"So you got some shit on your chest to get off LaLa. Say what you got to say so your nigga can fuck. I been ready to get back in them guts since I left earlier. You know the longer you make me wait for my pussy the worse it's gonna be for you."

He said that with a look that told me he was serious as hell. But the anticipation had my pussy wet already. So I was the opposite of worried.

"I'm ready to give us another try Messiah. I love you enough to see you're trying to do shit right this time. I want to be with you and I'm willing to try and trust you again. But you got to be the real ass nigga you promised me you would from the beginning. If this ain't what you want now or down the road just keep it real with me. Don't have me thinking we're something we're not. Don't have me out here looking like a fool over you. I'm gonna always love you, but I won't put up with you fucking around on me and if we're gonna do this you gotta be all the way in."

Messiah made me feel like I could breathe again. He showed me the possibility of a life filled with love. We were having a baby together and building something special. All I wanted was to be his rock. Someone he could depend on and hold him down no matter what came his way. I just needed him to do the same for me. I hoped I didn't regret giving him another chance later on, but that was a chance I willing to take.

Messiah (Money)

Larissa told me she was willing to give me another chance and that shit had me feeling on top of the fuckin' world. She was who I depended on to keep me sane with the life I lived. When shit got hectic in the streets she always brought me peace at home and I appreciated her more for that. We shared a bond that I knew I would never have or want with another woman. She was it for me.

I thought about what she was saying and looked at her with nothing but love. Shit, this damn girl was my fucking world. She was everything I could want in a woman and she was willing to give a nigga another chance. There wasn't no way I was about to fuck this up. I wanted her to be my damn wife one day. I had enough respect for her to do what she was asking. When she asked me to keep shit a hundred with her and be the man I promised from the jump I knew this time I was ready.

"I got you ma, and I'm gonna live up to that shit this time. I love you Larissa and you been mine since day one. I'm all yours."

"Prove it nigga"

I leaned over LaLa and kissed her deep before pulling away.

"Take your clothes off and let daddy eat."

Larissa slowly took off her clothes one piece at time so I could enjoy each part of her body more. She was standing up in in front of me and I wanted to show her that I meant every fucking word I said. I stood over her and began sucking and kissing every inch of her body while she was standing. I took my time letting my hands massage her entire body as I made my way lower.

I got down on my knees and when I had her pussy in my face I spread her lips with my fingers while blowing on her clit. I started teasing her by running my tongue around every part except her clit or opening, driving her crazy as fuck. I went and laid down on the bed. She looked at me like I had lost my mind since I just stopped eating her pussy before I even really started.

"Come sit on my face. I want you to ride that shit"

She came and placed her knees next to my head on either side and before she lowered herself down onto my mouth I pulled her down and began going to work. She acted like I was sucking the life out of her and couldn't take the shit, so I grabbed her legs and spread her wider. Then I began moving her up and down to the rhythm I wanted her to be moving. She was screaming all types of shit and begging me to stop.

After her third time cumming I lifted her up and slid her right down my dick so she had this mothafuckin' monster all the way in. Her face was tense and I knew that shit was hurting. She looked like she was about to pass out. I wasn't letting her up though she was gonna take all this dick. Her pussy muscles had my shit stuck that's how tight the shit was clenching down.

"Ride this mothafucka and take this dick girl. Don't get scared now"

I slapped her ass hard as hell to get her moving. She started rotating her hips and bouncing her ass cheeks back and forth. Then she moved her legs up and her feet planted and began bouncing on my dick.

"Messiah, I love this dick. Fuck!"

I reached up and grabbed her titties squeezing them together. I brought her forward so I could suck on her hard nipples while she was still taking the dick. That shit had her going harder than before. She leaned her head backwards and arched her back with my hands cupping her breasts, still riding my dick. Her body started shaking and I made sure to grab her thighs and push my dick even deeper as we cummed together.

She collapsed on top of me with my dick still hard inside of her and I rubbed on her back until she finally got enough energy to move. We laid in bed talking about the baby while I smoked a blunt until I figured it was time to tell her about the surprise I had in store for her.

"LaLa I got a business meeting in Miami and we're flying out tomorrow. I want you to go to the salon and get all your shit done tomorrow and buy whatever you want at the mall you think you'll need. We'll be staying at least a week."

"But Messiah, you know I'm leaving for school in a couple days. I can't go with you."

"The fuck you mean you leaving for school. We just decided we're back together. How the fuck you gonna talk about leaving, especially while you got my seed growing inside you? That ain't happening period, so dead that shit."

"I have to go to college Money". LaLa complained.

"Aye, I'm tired of you calling me Money when you mad or don't get your way. To you I'm fucking Messiah. And you damn right you going to college, but you going right fucking here. Try me if you want to but I will drag your ass back if I have to. So get ready for the trip like I said shorty. It's not an option.

She didn't say shit after that and I could tell she was mad as hell. But fuck it, she told me to keep shit real with her and I was dead ass serious. She wasn't living separate from me for college or any other reason. She had to be out her damn mind if she thought she was.

LaLa might feel some type of way about it right now but she would get over it.

On top of everything else, I had enemies out there we hadn't even found yet so I had to keep her and my baby safe no matter what. I was a nigga that was hated by a lot of mothafuckas for the simple reason I was the nigga running these streets. Jealous fuck boys were always gonna come for what was mine and that included my fucking wife and kids.

Silk

Me and Draco were sitting in a rental car around the corner from our trap on the East side. It turned out the new little nigga that got promoted to lieutenant at this spot was official as hell. He gave us some valuable information about our trap getting hit.

It seemed there was some new nigga in town who came up from Miami recently and had been spending a lot of time with Brian's ass. Brian was the old lieutenant who got shot during the stick up. We didn't have no proof or anything yet but it was suspect as hell that this nigga appears in town only chilling with Brian's ass and right afterwards the trap he's in charge of gets hit. I would hate to think Brian was dumb enough to bite the hand that was feeding him but greed is a mothafucka.

So we were sitting out here keeping watch to see if there was any funny shit going on. We wanted to see what the fuck was up for ourselves now that Brian was released from the hospital today. We knew his ass would be by the trap sooner or later.

"There that nigga go right there." Draco pointed out.

Brian hopped out of the passenger seat of a new Mercedes that I had never seen before. He stopped by the driver's side window and said a few words to whoever was driving before heading in the house. It was obvious that Brian got hit pretty bad in the robbery. He was wearing a sling on his arm and looked like he had lost a lot of weight. His walk even seemed a little fucked up but that shit could have been from the pain meds he probably was on too.

In my eyes he should have done more to protect the dope and the money. This was kill or get killed out here and every thug knew that shit. Wasn't no way I would let a nigga leave without a trace from trying to pull a stick up on me. That seemed funny as hell to me. I mean didn't he have any heat on him? We always coached these niggas to be prepared at all times for anything to come their way. Shit just didn't add up.

The black Mercedes with that dark ass tint Brian had been riding in started driving away from the spot and happened to be coming in the direction we were parked. The car turned down the road we were parked on and I saw exactly who the mothafucka was who had robbed us. I would bet my life on that shit.

It was that same nigga Shanice was fucking with when I saw her at the restaurant the other day. I just hoped she wasn't in on this shit or unfortunately it would be lights out for her ass too even if I was feeling her.

"I know that nigga driving that damn Mercedes is the nigga who took our shit. I've seen him around before." I told Draco.

"Word. Let's get Brian's ass then so he can let us know more about the nigga." Draco replied with a smirk on his face.

He placed a phone call to the crew inside telling them to get that nigga for us and have his ass ready to be transported within the next hour. They would get his ass by any means necessary and we would take care of it from there.

About an hour later we had the crew meet us around ten miles away from our warehouse up North. We put that nigga Brian in the trunk and instructed our team go ahead back to the city. When we arrived to our property Money was already there waiting for us.

"Who would have thought you was a snake ass nigga Brian? We put your ass on and this how you repay us?"

Money was pacing back and forth like the ruthless ass nigga he was. We tied Brian to a chair with barbed wire so he could hardly move and if he did the wire would cut into his skin. We didn't gag his mouth because it was time to get some fucking answers from the snake.

I took the wire cutters I was holding and cut that niggas thumb off first. We needed his ass to talk and give us all the information on the mystery nigga who took our shit. He screamed out in pain but I had to make sure he was getting the fucking message. He was gonna die regardless but we could do this torture shit all day. So I went ahead and cut off another finger.

"Who's the nigga you're working with?" I asked straight out.

"Look, ya'll don't understand. I had no choice."

He began crying like the bitch he was. That shit made me even more mad because we had this fuck boy working for us. So I cut off another finger. I didn't care about his screaming and crying. None of that shit mattered. He crossed us and he knew the rules to the game.

"Fuck all that, we're not here for your excuses and shit. We need to know who the mothafucka is." I told his ass.

"All I got is a name. They'll kill my whole family. Please, get this shit over with." he was fading out of consciousness fast.

"His name!" Money yelled.

"Torio."

167

Two shots to the head from Draco had that snake slumped over. We went ahead and cleaned shit up the usual way giving us plenty of time to figure out how we were gonna find this nigga. All we really had was a name but I also knew Shanice would be able to put us in touch with the nigga.

Thinking about the night we fucked at the restaurant had my dick hard and ready to hit again. Shanice's pussy fit my dick perfectly and the connection between us was different than what I had experienced with any of these other bitches out here. When we were finished up at the warehouse it was already morning and the sun was starting to come up.

"Come outside. I need you to ride with me real quick. It's important."

I was outside of Shanice's house and had to get her to agree to come with me. She came outside about five minutes later in some tight ass black leggings and an oversized off the shoulder grey shirt. Her hair was up and she was rocking some big ass sunglasses. My dick was ready to feel her pussy again but that shit had to wait until after business.

She sat down in my ride and I drove off. As I was driving, I couldn't help thinking about the bitch ass nigga that she had been fucking with and the fact he was the same mothafucka who stole from us. I was getting more and more heated about the shit and at this girl next to me. Shanice should have never been with another nigga, let alone that nigga. What the fuck was she thinking downgrading to him and trying to play me? I drove around for a minute until I calmed down. Then I finally pulled over at a nearby park so we could talk.

"Shanice I'm only gonna ask you this shit one time and you better tell me the fucking truth."

"Nigga..." she started but quickly stopped talking when she saw that I had my 38 pulled out pointed at her.

"Who was that nigga you was with the other night at the restaurant and how you know him?"

"His name is Torio. I just met him like a month ago over at my cousin Brian's house. We linked up and been messing around. But why the fuck you gotta pull a gun on me over some nigga?"

She said in one breath which showed me she wasn't trying to hide anything. She was telling the truth. I liked how the gun didn't seem to put any fear in her heart though. She didn't even flinch when she saw that shit, which proved she was the type of woman I needed in my life.

"I had to make sure you wasn't on some snake shit shorty. We good now."

I said while I leaned over and started kissing her before taking off her sunglasses and setting them aside. She didn't resist which let me know to keep going.

"Come here Shanice."

I needed to fuck. After a kill my adrenalin was always on ten until I got some pussy. She took off her pants leaving her shirt on and climbed over the seat into my lap while facing front. She knew exactly what the fuck I wanted. I saw her fat ass in my face and grabbed that shit with both hands.

"Pull that dick out Silk. My pussy is dripping wet ready for it."

I put two fingers in her pussy and one in her ass to see how wet she really was and her juices were coating my hand. I began moving them in and out of her while she was still bent over the steering wheel in front of me.

I reclined the seat all the way back to give us more room. With my other hand I slid my pants down low enough until my dick sprang out. Then I brought her pussy right down on it.

She began bouncing up and down holding onto the steering wheel for support while I kept both hands gripping her ass cheeks. I wanted to see every fucking thing. Her pussy was making sucking noises each time she came down on my dick and not long after I let my nut fill her up while she was cumming back to back. We stayed how we were for a minute with her still on my hard dick before finally getting ourselves together.

"Damn girl, you know shit's official now. Ain't no more running from this shit. You handle my dick like it's yours." I said to break the silence.

"Whatever nigga. We can try talking again and see where it goes but I'm leaving for college this week. So it can't be nothing serious. Plus you out here pulling guns on me and shit. Nah I'm good."

"We'll see. But I need you to do me a favor."

She rolled her eyes. Damn if we had more time I would fuck her again just to put her damn attitude in check, but this shit needed to be handled right away.

"Call that nigga Torio and have him meet you somewhere. I need to talk to him."

I didn't want to give her any details, because even though she made it sound like what they had was nothing, I didn't know if she had any feelings for the nigga. I didn't think she did if she fucked me while they was out on a date but I couldn't take that risk.

"Okay" Shanice agreed.

She took her phone out and set that shit up. She planned on meeting with him for lunch. We had a few hours before I would have the nigga right where I wanted him. I was gonna take her back to my place first. It was time I stopped taking it easy on her ass and showed her what my dick game was really all about. We only had a couple quickies so far but now I was gonna take my time with her.

Torio

That bitch Shanice must have thought I was a dumb ass nigga. She called me after not talking to me for over a week to meet up all the sudden. Not to mention, I was moving ten steps ahead of Money and his crew. I was raised for this type of shit. I was taught to know my enemies before showing my hand. They thought I was some small time fuck boy who had come here to hit a quick lick out of jealousy or greed. They had no idea how deep this shit ran.

I did that shit to let them see how easy it was for them to be touched. The stupid niggas walked around here without a care in the world. They weren't used to being as big as they were trying to be and were outa their fuckin' leauge.

I rolled over on top of the bitch I was currently laid up with. She was another part of my plan and it seemed like shit was coming together perfect. I pressed my dick against her ass and knew she liked all that freaky shit. So I took my other hand and spit on it then rubbed it right on her ass crack before I stuck my dick in with ease. Her asshole had been blown out way before me. She was just another typical hoe out here.

The bitch started to wake up from her sleep and began moving her ass back taking this dick. I wasn't no small nigga either. My dick was thick and long. I began going harder and then pulled out to bust on her back. I didn't have time to love on these hoes. They could catch my nut and suck my dick but that was about it. They knew what I wanted from the beginning.

Shorty got up out of the bed and went to get in the shower. I heard her baby crying and knew she did too but the shit didn't seem to phase her. She just went ahead and got in the shower anyway. I walked in the bathroom and got in the shower with her.

She got down on her knees and went to work sucking my dick. She was deep throating my dick before I even washed her ass off me. She was happy as hell to be down on her knees taking another nut. Once we got out I started putting my plan in motion on her end.

"So baby, I was thinking I could take you to Miami with me and we could be a family down there."

"Really Torio? You know I love you. So don't play with me."

"I'm serious as hell. You're everything a nigga could want. I love your ass too girl." I said gassing her head up with shit.

"When can we leave?"

"As soon as you make sure Monae's father isn't gonna be a problem then we can head out. Shit, you know I'm on probation and can't be having the nigga bringing heat to me right now. I want you, me and baby girl to be a real family without that fuck nigga getting in the way."

"I'll take care of Money you don't have to worry about him." She said exactly what I wanted to hear.

I put my clothes on and got the hell up out of there. I wanted to see Shanice's face when I didn't show up to the little lunch date she planned. I needed to see who had been in her ear about me in the first place. I had to admit shorty was a good fuck. Her pussy was tight and she could take the dick. She wasn't as bad as Money's bitch though. I understood why he was crazy behind her ass and she was loyal as fuck. After I saw the shit Shanice had set up I planned on catching a flight. It was time for me to touch back down in the 305 and keep shit moving forward.

Larissa

I tried to get up with Shanice this morning so she could go with me to get my nails done and hit the mall but her phone was turned off and went straight to voicemail. I don't know why Messiah insisted I go to the salon to get my hair done when he knew I didn't trust bitches to fix my hair right. I was gonna go though and if my hair ended up fucked up it would be his fault.

I made my way down to this salon that I heard was really good with different styles and cuts. Since I was here I might as we go all out and make a drastic change. I sat down in the stylist's chair who seemed nice enough and let her know that I wanted a slanted bob with some red highlights. I figured at least my new hair would surprise Messiah if nothing else.

After my hair was washed and the stylist, whose name was Kamia, began cutting my hair I started texting Shanice's ass since she just now decided to get up with me. I told her I was getting my hair done and wanted to see her when I was done since Messiah had us flying out to Miami tonight. I needed to tell her about the change of plans for school and it was better to let her know everything in person.

Messiah put his foot down last night. I wasn't upset about staying here instead of going away for school. I did feel like a bad friend though since me and Shanice made all these plans. I hoped she understood and didn't feel some type of way about it.

As I looked in the mirror to see the results of my new hair style I couldn't help but be pleasantly surprised. I was actually really feeling the new look and was excited to show it off to Messiah. Shanice and I decided to meet at a restaurant that was about a block away. I was looking forward to seeing her because since moving back in with Messiah I hadn't gotten to spend much time with my best friend. We spoke to each other on the phone all the time but it felt good to be on my way to meet up with her.

When I arrived, the restaurant was pretty busy. I told the hostess I needed a table for two and was ushered to a corner table. A few minutes later Neesy arrived.

"Oooooh bitch, I love your hair! You're on your grown and sexy shit now I see." Shanice said as soon as she sat down.

"Thanks friend. I was trying to have you come with me today so you would know all the juicy details of my life but you were MIA." I replied back.

"Sorry girl, I got caught up with a dumb ass nigga and was trying to help him out."

"Well how did that go for you? I also wanted to let you know that I was flying out to Miami tonight. Messiah is taking me with him on a trip while he takes care of business."

"That nigga had me on a wild goose chase today. But enough about that... I'm so glad you finally got your shit together and are taking another chance. Money must be doing something right! Plus he's taking you on a trip, you been putting that pregnant pussy on his ass."

She was being all extra and I couldn't do anything but laugh.

"Yeah something like that. So who was this man you were trying to help out? I questioned. I could tell that she was trying to avoid telling me the details and I wasn't going for it.

"Silk... We kind of hooked back up too! Damn, why does that nigga have to be so sexy? He has some kind of pull on me and I don't want to get in a situation like last time."

"Girl obviously you two have some unfinished business and like you told me you can't be scared of getting hurt. You have to just go with it and see what happens. And what do you mean again?"

"Oh shit, I forgot to tell you about the bathroom. Bitch can you believe I pulled a hoe move and left the nigga I was out on a date with and fucked Silk in the bathroom. I don't even operate like that, that's why I'm even more scared. I've never been open like he got me and I can't be out here stupid for a nigga." Shanice confided in me.

"I understand Neesy, but maybe you should give him a real chance and see. I mean you're already fucking!" I said with a smile.

I thought Shanice was being too hard on herself. She didn't sleep around at all and I definitely understood how a man could have you doing things you never thought you would. We finished our lunch and parted ways. She was still planning on leaving to go away to school and said she understood that I needed to stay here since I was back with Money and we had a baby on the way.

On the way home home I decided to stop by the store and pick up some rotisserie chicken since that was what I was craving. I had just begun to have cravings and when I had a taste for something nothing else would satisfy it. I was only a couple of months pregnant so my body hadn't changed except my ass and breasts had gotten a little bigger.

While I was waiting in line a nice looking light skinned nigga came and stood behind me but was close enough I could smell his expensive cologne. When it was my turn, I put my order in then went and stood to the side to wait for the food to be ready.

"Shorty, why you in here picking up your own food? Your man should be doing that shit for you."

I heard the same man that had been standing behind me say. I turned to give him a polite smile without responding. I didn't want to be rude, but I also wouldn't disrespect Messiah and be out here holding a conversation with another nigga. When I turned around the nigga actually caught my attention for a second which was surprising because Messiah was the only other man who ever really had any type of effect on me.

This man was tall and light skinned with a strong build and tattoos on his arm. What caught me off guard was his dark eyes. It was just something about them that had me staring into them. I quickly turned back around once I realized that I made eye contact for too long. The last thing I wanted to do was send the wrong message and have him thinking I was interested. Shit I was definitely off the market and didn't want this man to think I was available.

"I can see you got a nigga and you're not trying to give me any of your time. That shit is a turn on ma and I can respect that. My name's Torio. Hopefully that nigga will fuck up and I'll see your fine ass again." He said while my back was still turned to him.

"We all can hope."

I didn't even turn back around when I responded this time because last time was so awkward. My order was ready so I grabbed my chicken and left without another look.

Once I got inside the house I tore into the chicken and fixed Messiah a plate with some left over sides we had in the refrigerator. He walked in the front door shortly after and made his way over to me.

"Damn you're new look got my dick hard already."

"Stop playing Messiah, you know that big ass dick stay hard thinking about me". I teased, even though his dick really was always hard when he was around me.

"But we don't got time for that. Your ass needs to wait until we land in Miami. I fixed you a plate and then we can head out after you eat."

"Alright I'll eat what you fixed but I'm eating your pussy before we leave and you know I'm dead ass so you might as well walk your fine ass upstairs and take off them clothes now. I'm about to have your ass begging for the dick after. But you not getting any now until we land like you said with all that shit you talking."

"Whatever Messiah, you know I won't be begging for shit."

Since I knew he was serious as hell I did take my ass upstairs and get ready for daddy. I was ready for him to eat my pussy and have me cumming back to back. A few minutes later Messiah entered the room and walked over to me where I was positioned with my legs open wide. I was already playing in my pussy.

"I'm ready daddy. You want your dessert right?"

"Damn right I'm about to dive in that shit and get every drop."

He got down on his knees and pulled my pussy right into his face like it was his favorite meal. He started sucking on my clit and I climaxed right away.

"See this shit LaLa, you're pussy fuckin' dripping."

He went back to work while looking up at me using his tongue to bring on another orgasm before he decided I had enough. I tried to get his pants off and free his dick but he pushed my hands away and walked out of the room. That was some childish shit he was doing now. He got me ready for the dick, just to mess with my head. Two could play at the game though. I would show his ass and I had the perfect thing in mind.

After packing the car and going straight to the private jet Messiah booked, we were on our way. It was only us and the flight staff on the plane. I began rubbing on Messiah's dick through his pants while he was on the phone with Draco talking business. He had on some sweats so I was able to get a good grip and was stroking it. He shot me a look like he didn't want me to start some shit but he should have known better than the childish shit he pulled earlier.

Before he had a chance to stop me I pulled at his pants and released his dick from his boxers. I was stroking his dick nice and slow while applying some pressure. I took off my leggings and climbed over onto his lap so that I was straddling him with my pussy just touching the tip of his dick. Messiah was still on the phone and I knew he was discussing some important shit which made my mission even better.

I raised up and let his dick sink into my pussy. Once I was completely settled with him filling me up, I sat there staring into his eyes. I clenched my pussy muscles and moved around in circular motions. I was enjoying the sight of his facial expressions. He was trying to hold it together and finish the conversation but I knew he wanted to fuck the shit out of me with the way I was moving and had him feeling.

All of the sudden I raised up off of his dick and hopped off his lap. I put my leggings back on and sat my ass back down next to him like nothing ever happened. He was staring a hole in me but I refused to make eye contact with him, so he squeezed my thigh hard as hell causing me to look over at him and smile big as hell. I knew I had gotten him good but shit he left me without the dick so now he knew how that shit felt. After he ended the phone call he was on my ass.

"LaLa why you trying me ma. You know I'm gonna fuck up your life when we touch down. You not gonna be able to walk the entire fucking week for that shit right there."

He grabbed his dick to adjust himself even though I knew it wouldn't help. He got to feel the pussy and not get his nut out. So I didn't doubt the punishment he had in store for me. But that only had me more than ready for us to land.

I had never been to Miami before or even Florida. I was enjoying the scenery as we made our way to the hotel we were staying at. Of course Messiah pulled out all the stops and booked an expensive ass hotel and big ass suite. He never was over the top with spending money, except when it came to me. I didn't ask him for anything but I appreciated the thought he put into the shit that concerned me.

I was fine without all the nice things and expensive gifts. I loved Messiah for who he was not what he could do for me. He always told me to accept the things he bought me and that it was just another way he showed his love for me. I had to admit it was nice to have someone put me first and let me know that they would do anything to put a smile on my face.

I was soaking in the tub because my pussy was so sore from Messiah putting it on me when we first arrived at the hotel. He wouldn't even let me unpack. As soon as he closed the door to the suite we fucked all over the place. I was paying for it now though and knew that my walk would be different for at least a day. His dick was just that big. Every Time we had sex I had to get used to his size all over again and that curve had my insides rearranged at this point probably.

Carina

I needed to get away from North Carolina and move on with my life. Torio was ready to become a family and it was the perfect time. That dumb nigga Money dropped me for his new bitch and I wasn't about to be left out here nickel and diming turning tricks to live. I didn't mind doing some shit on the side but I wanted a certain type of lifestyle and tricking wasn't paying for the shit I wanted. That nigga Torio though, he kept my pockets full. Since I started fucking with him I was able to get my hair and nails done on the regular and go on shopping sprees whenever I wanted.

There wasn't no way I was letting him get away. All he wanted was for me to handle Money so that I would be able to take Monae with me. I wasn't stupid though. Money was a real thug out here in the streets and his ass was capable of anything. Trying some shit with him would end bad for me. So I figured what Torio didn't know wouldn't hurt him. I used up all of my remaining funds and booked the next flight to Miami. Torio had already left for Miami and told me whenever I finished my business here with Money to make my way down so we could be together.

"I'm here baby." I sung into the phone while I was standing outside of the baggage claim after my plane landed.

"Word, where you at?" Torio asked.

"I'm at the airport. I need you to come get us."

"Bet. I'll be there soon."

After waiting a little over an hour Torio pulled up in a nice ass red Lamborghini. This nigga really had all my attention with the type of dough he was bringing in.

When he pulled up to the curb, I put my luggage in the trunk and sat the baby's car seat in the back before getting into the front seat next to my man.

After I closed the door I leaned over the seat and started kissing all over Torio. I let my hand slide into his pants and began rubbing on his dick. The other thing I loved about this nigga was his dick. He wasn't as big as Money but he was still big. He was a nasty mothafucka too and liked to do all types of shit.

"I'm so glad I'm here Torio. You know I couldn't stay away long." I said while I continued rubbing his dick picking up the pace. He took my hand and pulled it out of his pants which surprised the hell out of me. He focused back on driving like the shit was nothing, even with his dick hard. A few minutes later he finally spoke up.

"So you took care of your baby daddy? I don't want shit to be hot my way over that nigga."

"Yeah, I took care of it. You got nothing to worry about. So where we staying baby?"

"I'm about to drop you and Monae off at the hotel and I'll swing by later." He said, not even looking my way.

"Oh, I thought we was staying with you. But that's cool I guess."

I didn't have much of a choice and I wasn't about to go back to NC, so I would make the shit work. He was the one footing the bill anyway. When we pulled up to the hotel I was in awe. At least the nigga was putting us up in a nice ass hotel. The shit was amazing. He must really be in love to spend this type of money. Once inside I went to the front desk to check in like Torio told me to do and then began walking over towards the elevator. The elevator door opened and I about lost my fucking mind.

I saw Money and that stupid bitch he left me for all cuddled up in the corner. The worst part was he had his hands down her pants like it wasn't nothing. Like her pussy was a fucking treasure or some shit and he was looking at her with nothing but love. He never looked at me like that the entire four years I had known his ass. I began crying hysterically and that's when the two mothafuckas finally noticed the goddamn door was open and they weren't alone.

Money didn't care that I standing in front of him one bit. It was the exact opposite. To make it worse he rubbed that shit in my face. He pushed the button to hold the door open and smiled at me. Right after, he took his other hand out of that hoe's pussy and began sucking her juices off his fingers. Never had that nigga done anything like that to me and that's when I realized he didn't give a fuck about me. Shit, he probably never gave a fuck about me which hurt me to the core since I really gave that nigga my heart.

The elevator doors closed and I swear I could hear that bitch laughing like shit was funny. I knew I would get the last laugh though. One way or another they both would pay.

Larissa

We had been in Miami for two days and spent most of our time in the hotel fucking. But today I convinced Messiah we needed to get out of this hotel. He was going to take me shopping and then he told me he had a surprise for me later. I kept trying to get him to tell me what the surprise was but he wouldn't budge. As we were getting ready to leave I couldn't help but to admire my man.

From his dark skin, dreads, down to his wide shoulders and muscles. He was too damn sexy and he was all mine. Every Time I looked at him I swear I fell more in love. I knew bitches swarmed him every day and so far he had proven to me that I was all he wanted. He showed me more and more every single day why I loved him so much. He wasn't a perfect man, but he was the right one for me.

I was looking at this fine boss ass nigga who I could claim as my own, and for once in my life felt like I was ready to let him completely in. It was time for me to love with no reservations. I understood we were still young but I felt like he truly was my soulmate and now that we were starting a family together everything just seemed even more right.

I decided to wear a turquoise maxi dress with a wrap-around look that had a slit up to the thigh for the day. I chose some gold sandals to match and decided not to wear any jewelry. Since getting my new hairstyle I liked to keep the jewelry simple to none. My hair was drastic enough with the cut and color. I wanted to look extra sexy for my man since he really stepped up with this trip. Everything had been absolutely perfect so far.

"Damn LaLa where you going like that? You better got something on under that shit."

"Whatever Money!" I rolled my eyes playfully and began walking towards the door.

"Alright Larissa, you know who the fuck I am. Keep that fuckin' attitude shorty or I'll really fuck you up." He said loud as hell while grabbing at his crotch.

The whole hotel probably heard what he said since he was holding the door wide open. He gave zero fucks about anything, but I loved his ass anyway. When I brushed against him while walking out the door, he pushed me right back into the room.

"Take your ass out on the balcony LaLa."

"But Messiah…" I started to protest but he cut me off.

"I don't wanna hear that shit. You know how I get down ma."

Our suite had a nice balcony. It overlooked the ocean on one side and came all the way around the side of the hotel to the street side. There was a table out there and some nice beige and black colored outdoor furniture.

"Go over to the railing right there." Messiah pointed to the part of the balcony over by the street.

I knew he was up to some slick shit. I could see he was serious as hell though so I took my ass right over to the spot he was pointing at. I leaned back against the railing while facing my man waiting for him to tell me what he wanted me to do now. Messiah was a boss in every sense of the word. He loved when I was obedient and let him be in control and I loved that shit too.

He came over to where I was standing and leaned in close so I could feel every inch of his body even with the clothes between us.

"Turn around." He demanded, so I did just that.

187

I placed my hands on the rail and watched the busy street below. We were ten floors up and the street was filled with people. There was even people out on the other balconies at our hotel and a plenty others were outside at the hotel next to us. I was enjoying the view when I felt the ocean breeze on my ass and my pussy.

Messiah lifted up my dress so that he had a perfect view of my bald pussy and bare ass, while others from below or around us couldn't see a damn thing. I heard his pants drop and knew he was really about to have sex with me out here on the balcony. Messiah liked public sex and didn't care who was around. He felt like he owned the "mothafuckin' world" as he said, and could do whatever he wanted whenever he wanted. Shit, I wasn't about to argue with him. His dick could have me doing any and everything he said.

"You must have been waiting for me to fuck you. You got all my shit out like this."

He said while sticking his fingers inside me and moving them around stretching me wide. I threw my ass back and started making it clap to really get him excited. He began gripping it and slapping my ass turning me on more. I loved when he was rough and left marks. He used his hands to push my legs farther apart before he put his dick in and started going to work.

Here I was on the balcony bent over taking this nigga's monster dick and I loved every minute of it. I began moaning and continued popping my ass while he was deep inside me.

"Damn girl throw that shit back. Take your dick ma."

"Messiah you better fuck me nigga. You're playing right now."

I said trying to prove a point. He wasn't satisfied with how hard he could dig in me after I said that. So he

188

lifted me up and sat me down on the table after pushing all the shit that was on top of it onto the ground. He ripped my dress off from the top to the bottom like it was nothing, so now I was completely exposed.

He grabbed my breasts roughly and pulled them into his mouth as he leaned down. He started biting on my nipples making sure to give me some pain while he was rearranging my damn insides with his dick. I was in heaven with how he was putting it on me and cummed all over his dick. I looked down and saw my juices as he moved in and out of me. I reached down and played with my clit.

"I'm not done yet. You gonna take this mothafuckin' dick LaLa."

He began pounding my pussy and when I couldn't take it anymore he lifted both my legs straight up in the air and spread them apart into a V. My pussy got even tighter on his dick but he wouldn't slow down.

"Oh God, Messiah I can't take it no more!"

"You better not cum until I tell your ass to either."

I was trying my best to keep that shit in but he was hitting every single spot. His dick was so big it had my walls clenching down more and more while I tried to hold back my orgasm. Messiah's whole body tensed up and all at once he let everything go. As he finished releasing inside me I squirted all over his dick and soaked the table.

After washing each other and getting ready for a second time we walked hand in hand as we left the hotel. At least this time we didn't crosss paths with that nasty bitch Carina. I can't believe she followed us down to Miami which left me wondering what she had up her sleeve. Messiah told me not to worry about her and that she wasn't a threat to us because he didn't want her in any way.

I believed him but I also wasn't about to underestimate her either. She had to be up to something for her to come all the way down to Miami while we were here and on top of it she was staying at the same hotel. I knew she was up to something and I wasn't putting anything past her.

Messiah took me shopping like he promised but we mostly walked around looking in different tourist shops rather than buying much of anything. I was glad to spend time with him where I didn't have to share him with the streets. That was the best part of the trip so far. When the sun began to set Messiah had the driver take us back to the hotel. I wondered what he was really up to, but decided to go with it. When the car stopped Messiah got out first and held his hand out for me to take as I stepped out of the car. He led me down to the bar inside the hotel and told me he had to leave and take care of something real quick. He went ahead and ordered me a drink while I waited.

I was sitting at the bar enjoying my lemonade when a man sat down next to me.

"Hey shorty, you believe in that fate shit right?"

I turned to see who the nigga was since he acted like he knew me. To my surprise it was the same man who tried running game on me a few days ago at the grocery store back home. I already knew this was some suspect shit so my guard went up right away.

"Are you stalking me nigga? This seems like too much of a coincidence to me, Torio was it." I replied to his comment about fate.

I was serious as hell too. What were the chances of seeing this same nigga at a grocery store and now at the same hotel I was at hundreds of miles away from home.

"See you remember my name. I could tell you wanted the dick". He said that shit like it was a joke.

I had on a short dress and the creepy ass man decided to put his hand on my exposed thigh.

"But for real I live out here. I was up in NC visiting my fam. But the shit does seem funny as hell huh?"

I suddenly felt a presence behind me and could tell from how my body responded that it was Messiah. I cringed and started almost shaking because this random nigga's hand was still on my thigh. So I knew Messiah was about to flip the fuck out.

I heard the sound of a click and the man's hand instantly moved away from my thigh. I turned in my chair to see exactly what was going on and when I did, I saw Messiah with a dark look in his eyes holding a pistol to the man's head. The man was staring right at Messiah without an ounce of fear while he had a hand on his back, probably where he had a gun too.

"This right here is mine nigga. Fuck you doing putting your hands on my damn wife?" Messiah spoke like the boss he was.

"My bad bruh, we good. I didn't know. No worries she wasn't going for it anyway."

Torio said without moving an inch except to wink at me. He must have had a death wish I swear or he didn't know who he was dealing with. Messiah took the butt of his gun and hit him upside the head back to back. Torio spit out blood and just sat there looking crazy as hell but not seeming phased in the least. I backed my chair away to keep out of the way.

Messiah looked like he was a completely different person right now. This was the side of him I never fully witnessed but knew was there. Torio finally stood up and began walking towards the door with his hand now holding his weapon. He kept facing Messiah while backing out, never turning his back.

"Shorty remember to get up with me when your nigga fuck up."

That stupid nigga yelled at me like I really knew who he was. At that moment a flash of hurt and hatred crossed Messiah's face as his eyes met mine. I could tell he really believed something was going on between me and that Torio nigga. Once he left the bar area, Messiah grabbed my arm and pulled me towards the doors that led out to the beach.

By now it was dark outside and the stars and moon were shining brightly. Messiah was dragging me out and I was stumbling to keep up. As we approached the beach I saw a pathway lit with candles in jars and a tent set up. He kept pulling me until we were in front of a table set for two which I assumed was his surprise for me tonight.

I was in tears at this point because I saw the anger on his face and understood it was directed at me. Messiah had never been upset with me and even though I hadn't done anything wrong, Messiah believed I had something going on with that man.

"You see this shit LaLa? You got a nigga ready to go to war for you and you're nothing but a fucking slut. You with the next nigga the minute I step away. Look at this shit Larissa. I was gonna fucking propose to you tonight. I thought you was my mothafuckin' ride or die, my damn soulmate and you fucking played me."

I stood there crying. I wasn't crying because I had done anything wrong. I was crying because Messiah must have really felt that way towards me if he could sit here and say that shit like I was nothing to him.

"Messiah, I don't know that man." I was crying uncontrollably now and began walking away. I had to get out of there.

"Nah, you not about to walk away from this shit LaLa."

"Yes the fuck I am Messiah. You out here calling me out of my name disrespecting me. That shows me how you really feel nigga. You don't love me. I'm done."

He tried to grab my arm to keep me from leaving but I pulled away and kept walking. I just wanted to get up to the hotel room and get away from him as soon as possible. He could get another room or go wherever the fuck he wanted. There was no way I was gonna let him treat me like shit or disrespect me especially when I didn't do anything wrong. He should know me better than that. I closed the hotel room door and laid down crying until I fell asleep.

Messiah (Money)

I fucked up tonight, and I hated that I treated LaLa like shit. She was my fucking world and here I was calling her names and jumping to conclusions. When I walked up and saw another nigga's hands on her I saw red and I lost fucking control. Shit I almost committed murder in a room full of people and would do that shit again in a heartbeat. That's how Larissa had me. I don't even think she realized how much I loved her or that I would do anything for her.

I was ready to ask her to be my wife and spend the rest of my life with her. She was my everything and now she wasn't even trying to be around me. I went ahead and booked another hotel room next to our suite for the night. LaLa was pregnant and didn't' need to be stressed out behind my bullshit right now so I would let her rest tonight and make it up to her tomorrow. I didn't know how I was gonna make it up to her but I was ready to do anything to get on her good side again. I undressed and smoked the blunt I had from earlier before finally falling to sleep with the shit that happened heavy on my mind.

I woke up and noticed my phone was damn near dead because my charger was in our suite next door. I went into the hallway and let myself back into our room. LaLa was still passed out asleep in the bed looking beautiful. She had my heart completely and I would kill any mothafucka who laid a finger on her.

I walked up to the bed and put my hand on her stomach. To feel my son growing inside of her made me feel whole. She moved in her sleep some and after I placed a kiss on her forehead I made sure to stay quiet as I grabbed my charger for the car. I had an important business meeting with the connect this morning and needed to get going so I wouldn't be late.

I jumped in the shower and got ready fast as hell and within fifteen minutes I was leaving out of the room again while LaLa was still sleeping. The spot we were meeting up at was a small restaurant about ten blocks away. Just before I pulled up and parked I sent Larissa a text letting her know I was sorry and we would talk later. I wanted her to know I was thinking of her even if we weren't on good terms. What we had was forever so we would have to work this shit out no matter what, whether she wanted to or not.

I walked into the restaurant which was completely empty except for two people sitting at a table with their backs to me. I made my way over to the table assuming it was Fe and took a seat. When I sat down I was pissed the fuck off. I saw the connect and that same nigga I almost bodied last night for touching LaLa sitting together. Instantly my instincts were telling me this was some bullshit and these niggas were on some other shit.

I was wishing I had brought more heat and backup for the meeting. Right now they had me stuck in a bad situation. I tensed up and I'm sure my anger was written all over my damn face.

"What's this Fe?" I got straight to the point.

"I wanted you two to meet up so you can start working together. Money this is Torio, Torio this is Money." He said as he introduced us.

"Nice to meet you." That dumb ass nigga Torio said with a smile on his fucking face.

I wasn't feeling this shit at all so I let it be known. Not only had I already wanted to kill this nigga for touching my wife but come to find out he was the same mothafucka who had hit my trap and got away. This had to be a set up.

"I met this fuck nigga last night when he had his hands on my wife. He's also the same nigga that's got some slugs with his name on them for stealing my shit. Fe, I respect you, but I'm not working with a bitch ass nigga whose days are numbered. I'm out."

I stood up and began walking out leaving them both sitting there watching me go. There wasn't any way I was gonna believe this shit happened by chance. I was gonna get that nigga Torio though, he had to go.

Larissa

I woke up upset from not seeing Messiah next to me. I remembered the argument we had and felt sad all over again. Then I looked at my phone and saw that he sent me a message so I relaxed somewhat. We still had to figure out this shit but at least he was sorry and ready to move forward. I was willing to forgive him because last night he completely lost it and was talking out of anger. We both said some shit we didn't mean but it wasn't anything we couldn't get past.

I got out of the bed and started getting ready for the day. I could tell that Messiah came in and got ready in the room this morning. I remembered he had the meeting this morning with his connect. So I decided to order room service for brunch because I had slept so late and was starving.

I called downstairs and ordered a full meal with pancakes, eggs, sausage and orange juice. While I was waiting I went ahead and jumped in the shower to freshen up for the day. I gained a few more pounds but I still wasn't showing at all yet. It was still too early in the pregnancy for that. I stood in the mirror turning sideways trying to imagine what I would look like with a huge stomach that I knew was coming.

I was really happy about having a child with Messiah. Since meeting him my whole outlook on family changed. My parents fucking me over really had me wondering what type of parent I would be and they were the reason I was hesitant about keeping the baby in the first place. But Messiah reassured me that I wasn't them and that I was gonna be a good mother.

Me and him may argue and have our problems but I knew in my heart that he was more than just my man he was my family too. When I thought back on everything I went through since meeting him, there wasn't one time where he wasn't there for me when I needed him. He may be flawed but his love for me was real.

As I was looking in the mirror thinking about everything, I heard a knock at the door. I hurried to put my robe on so I could let room service in with my food. This baby was making me eat like crazy. It was like no matter how much food I ate I never felt full.

I tied my robe and hurried over to the door. When I opened it I was instantly caught off guard. But before I was able to say a word, I felt a burning sensation in my chest. It was the worst pain I ever felt in my life. I realized that I had been shot and I fell to the floor as everything went black.

Messiah (Money)

I left the restaurant and had to calm myself down before heading back to the hotel. I didn't want LaLa to see me this mad since she had already experienced enough of that last night. It was still pretty early so I drove around through the streets of Miami for a while. I really liked it down here and definitely could see our operation expanding all the way from North Carolina down to Miami.

I even had some family down here in the game so shit wouldn't be that hard. I was willing to put in the hard work and time to make it happen. I wasn't satisfied with running only the state. I wanted it all and was gonna find a way no matter what. I was a young boss ass nigga but I knew what the fuck I was doing.

Now that Fe put the demand on me working with that fuck nigga Torio I would have to reconsider working with him altogether. He had the best prices and our relationship had been good until this point so maybe shit would still work out. I would reach out to him tomorrow and see where his head was at. But there wasn't a man alive that put fear in my heart or made decisions for me. So if I had to find another connect, I would. Whether he liked that shit or not.

A call came through on my phone and I picked it up without looking at the number of who was calling. As soon as I hit the talk button there was a loud ass explosion that hit the back of the rental car I was driving. The impact alone caused my car to flip over and my body was thrown from the vehicle.

When I came to, I was laying on the ground. My head was pounding and I couldn't fucking move because my legs were all fucked up. I had a big ass gash on both my legs and my clothes were covered in blood. I reached up and felt another cut on my forehead but the shit didn't seem too bad.

When I looked around to take in my surroundings, I saw those fuck niggas Torio and Fe standing there both holding guns pointed at me. I wasn't a bitch no matter how much pain I was in. So I looked each of them dead in the eyes daring the niggas to pull the trigger. Then some other fucker hit me over the head from behind with what felt like a gun. The nigga began dragging me away while I lost consciousness again.

When I finally woke back up, it took a minute for my eyes to adjust to the dim light of where I was being held. I was in some kind of big ass cargo crate filled with boxes. They had me tied to a chair with my hands, feet and mouth bound. My entire body was hurting like a mothafucka but I couldn't focus on that shit. I needed to figure out what the fuck was going on. Obviously these niggas had some shit planned where they didn't want me dead yet otherwise they would have pulled the trigger when they had the chance.

After racking my brain trying to figure shit out, I came to the conclusion that they had me on a damn ship from the rocking motion. Where were those niggas taking me?

To Be Continued...

Made in the USA
Middletown, DE
05 April 2019